GEMMA

ISBN: 979-8-9921675-1-1
Library of Congress Control Number: 2024927167
Publication Date: December 15, 2024

Published by Patrick L. Wimsatt

This book is lovingly dedicated to my amazing wife, Angela, who's love and devotion has taught me the true meaning of love.

Table of contents

Chapter ONE: The Purchase

A Slave Girl

It's cold and raining. The grey sky descending an eerie fog over the damp ground. I'm shivering as I walk along. The square is filled with the normal noise and activities of people coming and going. I keep my head down to keep the rain out of my face. Color catches my eye to the left; unusual on such a morbid day, so I turn to see what it is. It's bright yellow, so I walk towards it out of curiosity. As I get closer, I see it's a girl, in what looks to be a large cage. About 18 years of age and beautiful. Her long brown hair contrasted against her yellow dress. She is shivering, dirty, and clearly has been crying. My heart is moved.

I look to the owner of the wagon and cage. "What did she do?" I ask.

"She is my slave. I fought and won her. She's a fine girl and will fetch much money in the western trade markets".

I do not know why but my heart is deeply moved. I look at the girl; she is full of anger and fear. "How much for the girl?" I ask.

The man laughs aloud and replies "My friend, this insolent creature, this thing of beauty, is beyond the reach of commoners such as yourself. Why would you want a slave girl?"

"My business with her is not of your concern. How much?".

The owner scratches his beard, clearly not prepared for such a request. "For you my friend, nine hundred Lyra."

"Nine hundred Lyra? Six months wages for a slave girl? You will be lucky to get half that for her in the west where girls are easily bought and sold as common as grain. And you must get there! It's a very long journey, filled with danger; you will be lucky if you and her survive. I will give you three hundred Lyra, right here, right now, and take her off your hands."

The man laughs. "Three hundred Lyra? Good sir for three hundred Lyra you can go buy a goat. This girl will bear many children." He turns to mount his wagon to leave.

"Wait! You and I both know I can buy a goat for fifty Lyra. And a goat will not kill me in my sleep nor try to run away. I will give you five hundred Lyra. You will spend much feeding her and transporting her to the western ports, and you may or may not sell her for more."

The man thinks. "Why do you want her so badly? Is she of relation to you?"

"I told you, my business with her is none of your concern. But no, she is of no relation of which I am aware. I do not know who she is nor where she is from."

"Six hundred Lyra, no less or I leave now. You are wasting my time. Six hundred Lyra in coin right now? You have this much money, commoner?"

I pull out a bag of gold coins and count out six hundred Lyra. "She is now mine, release her."

The old man scoffs in disbelief, but nods in agreement. "Very well. She is yours," he says. "But watch this one, she is feisty." He laughs as he unlocks the cage.

The girl looks at me, her anger intense. "I will kill you in your sleep," she says. I ignore her. She is cuffed, collared, and chained. I take the chain, the keys to her restraints, and offer her my hand to help her out of the cage. She pushes it aside and falls to the ground. Then she gradually kneels up and stands up, her legs weak from being in the cramped cage for so long. She scowls at me, her face is a mess, and her hair is wet and matted. Her dress is torn and muddy.

"Can you walk?" I ask.

"I can walk," she replies.

The old man grins and bids us farewell. He mounts his wagon, takes the money, and pulls away. "Good luck my friend, you're going to need it with that one." He says as he pulls away.

I take the chain attached to the steel collar around the girl's neck and begin to walk once more on my journey. The girl follows behind in silence, wondering who I am and what I want with her, knowing well what happens to slave girls. Most are put to work in the whore houses and expected to return a profit.

"I will die before I become a whore," she says.

I ignore her and keep walking. Soon we reach my home and enter.

An Evening of Trust?

Once inside I guide her to the living area and offer her to sit on the sofa. I go to start a fire in the fireplace to remove the damp chill. The stone walls of my home provide fantastic security, but truly little insulation from the elements. My home is not fancy. I have a few odds and ends, and some pictures on the wall. I live a simple life, but I keep the place clean and presentable.

She watches me, noting everything about me. I am a slender man, 24 years old, handsome, and strong. And apparently rich she whispers aloud. My hair is brown, my eyes are blue, and I weigh about 90kg she estimates.

She asks, "Where are we?"

"This is my home," I reply. I pour a drink and sit in the chair adjacent to her. "What is your name?" I ask.

"My name is Gemma. Why did you buy me?"

I sit and just look at her a few moments, contemplating what I have done. "I do not know why I bought you. I had no plans to buy a slave, nor have I ever owned a slave. Tell me, how old are you? Where are you from? Where are your parents?

Gemma looks down, tears welling up in her eyes. "I am 19 years of age. I do not know where my parents are. I was kidnapped by men on horses. They attacked our village, and I was taken and sold without anyone knowing. She takes a deep breath, trying to compose herself. I'm from a small village on the outskirts of the kingdom, Timbervale by name. It was peaceful there.... until those men came...until they took me. I am grateful that you have bought me and thus kept me near my home, but I will never be a slave. I am a strong fighter, and I will kill you the first chance I get."

I get the keys to her constraints from my pocket and approach her. "Well, before you send me to my demise, I suggest you listen to what I have to say." I lean down and unlock the cuffs binding her hands, and then release the collar from around her neck. Gemma rubs her wrists, and her neck, and sits in silence puzzled that she has been released by her captor.

"I mean you no harm Gemma. I'm not going to hurt you nor abuse you and I have no use for a slave." Gemma's eyes light up at my words. Her excitement clearly heard as she exclaims, "Then I am free to go?"

I wave my hand motioning her to listen. "I do not wish to harm you, but there a very many that will. You are a beautiful prize, as you were to that merchant who sold you to me. If I release you, someone else will just capture you again. And next time, I will not be there to save you."

"Save me? You think you saved me? You bought me! As a slave. And now you're holding me prisoner in this dark and musty place you call home. How have you saved me?" asks Gemma.

I realize she is young, brash, and a foolish girl, never having been away from her village most likely. "Had I not purchased you, you would still be in that cage on your way to the west facing who knows what. Or worse, you'd already be dead, as stronger men stole you from that merchant, using your body for their pleasure before gutting you and dumping you in a river somewhere. So yes, my dear, whether you want to admit it or not, I saved you. Not to mention it cost me six hundred Lyra to do so."

I continue, "You are not bound now. If you wish to flee, you may do so. But think of this…you could not stop them from taking you before, what makes you think you can stop them from taking you again? With your help, and a little luck, we may possibly be able to find your parents. But you have no idea the dangers we face."

Gemma is still angry and scared, even having been released from her bindings. She moves from the couch to my chair, kneeling and placing her forehead on my knee. She looks up at me with a mixture of fear and hope. "You would help me find my parents? Thank you, I don't want to be a slave, I want to go home. I miss my parents so much. I don't know how we'll find them, but I'll do anything to get back to them. Anything you ask of me." She begins to cry.

I place my hand on her head. "Very well, then I trust you will not try to kill me in my sleep tonight?"

She looks up again at me, tears streaming down her face. "I will not attempt to hurt you good sir."

"Very well. The next few days may be challenging. In public, it will be necessary for us to keep up the appearance that you are my slave. But here in my home, you are free, do you understand?" She shakes her head affirmatively and wipes the tears from her face, only making herself look worse as she smears the dirt she has accumulated. "Are you hungry?"

Gemma nods, her stomach growling at the mention of food. "Yes, I am hungry...thank you for your kindness. I've been in that cage for days with very little to eat."

"Come with me." We head to the kitchen to get her some food. The fireplace is now roaring, and the dampness and chill are gone. In the kitchen I show her to the pantry and ice chest. "You may have whatever you like. I don't cook anymore, but you are welcome to fix whatever. There are dishes in the cabinet, and utensils in the drawers."

She asks timidly, "Have you eaten sir? I can cook for us both."

"No, I have not. That would be kind of you. Just, no poison please."

Gemma looks at me and smirks, acknowledging my comment but still not trusting me. "No sir, no poison, you have my word." Gemma rummages around trying to determine what to fix. She finds meat, potatoes, some vegetables, and gets started. I leave her to do her thing and return to my study. She looks at her reflection in the window, realizing how dirty she still is and begins wiping the dirt from her face.

After about an hour Gemma comes in. "Food is ready, would you like me to place it in the dining room? It's a bit chilly in there."

"No, let's just bring some plates in here please."

Gemma nods, "Yes, that would be great. I couldn't find drinks; do you want water?" she asks.

"No, I will get us a bottle of wine from the cellar."

Gemma brings in two plates of food and sets it on the small table, then returns to get glasses. I look at Gemma and say "This looks amazing Gemma and smells even more amazing. Where did you learn to cook like this? I have not had a meal like this in a long time."

Gemma blushes and pours the wine "My mother taught me to cook." Tears well up in her eyes again at the thought of her mother. "I pray that someday I can cook for her again."

"Tell me more about your village, Timbervale," I suggest as we eat.

She replies. "Timbervale is small, just over one hundred of us. We harvest lumber for construction and stay remarkably busy. We are a peaceful community, filled with laughter and support. The forest has always provided our security and our livelihood. Until...until last week. They came out of nowhere, killing those who fought back. Capturing the rest. Because of my age and appearance, I was sold. Will you really help me find my parents?"

"Yes. I have no need for a slave and no desire to keep you prisoner. I saw you in that cage and my heart could not bear to see another one of our women transported out of the kingdom. We shall attempt travel back to your Timbervale then, when you are able, and return you to your home."

Gemma sets down her plate. "Oh, thank you sir. How will I ever repay you? We will sell lumber, and I will repay your six hundred Lyra." She is grateful for the food, but still very sad, cautious, and suspicious of me.

"No need to repay me. We must work to rebuild our kingdom from such savages as those who raided your village. I am sure it is the work of Alazaar. Do you know this name?"

"Yes, I have heard of Alazaar, the King's executioner they call him. A horrible, evil man." We pick up our plates and return them to the kitchen. "Come with me."

I walk Gemma to an empty room. "You may stay here. It's not much, but it's clean and the bed is comfortable. There are additional blankets and pillows in the closet. There is a fireplace. I shall start a fire for you." I step across the hall. "Here is a washroom. You can bathe and get out of those clothes. I will set out clothes for you. When you are finished, come and talk with me in the study."

Gemma's eyes are amazed at the sight of the washroom and a real bed. "Sir, I don't know what to say. I have never seen such luxury. Your kindness is beyond charitable. Thank you." I run a pail of water. "I will put this over the fire so your bath will be warm." She interjects.... "oh no, let me do that. It is I who should be drawing you a warm bath. But after days in that cage, I will accept your hospitality." She picks up the pail and heads to the fireplace. I follow behind, watching her. She is not afraid of work, which is clear.

Gemma lets the water in the pail get hot and carefully carries it back to the washroom. She pours it in the tub and adds cold water to her desire. She then looks around for towels, closes the door, gets out of her filthy dress, and steps into the tub. She is used to bathing in an icy river. The warm water is so soothing as she settles in it helps her relax a bit. She rests her head against the tub and closes her eyes, sliding down till she is neck deep in the water. Some of her apprehension washes away, and for the first time in a week, she feels somewhat safe. She eyes the bar of soap and proceeds to scrub all the dirt and grime off every inch of her.

Meanwhile, I go through some old women's clothes in my possession and try to find something she may wear. I take it to her room and place it folded on the guest bed. I'm not used to company and have never had the company of a young woman. I feel out of place, but my wish is that she can be comfortable. I then retrieve some wood and start a fire for her.

I yell through the door, "Gemma there are clothes on your bed that I hope you will find suitable. Please take your time and relax. There is no hurry."

Gemma yells back through the door, "Thank you again, so much."

I return to the study and after stoking the fire, pour myself another glass of wine. I sit and contemplate what I have done. My mind runs wild: What will my friends say that I bought a slave girl? What if we cannot find her parents? How will she be treated in public? Folks here will only see her as a slave girl.

Gemma can't believe where she is, the meal she just ate, and the warmth of the water against her skin. She has never known such comfort. The bathroom is large, but the hot bath warms the whole room. She knows this is only for a night or two as she is determined to get back to Timbervale and her people, but for now she is grateful for this man that she does not know.

Her thoughts turn to her host. Who is he? What are his intentions? Is he really this kind or am I to be sold again? Or worse, will he come to my room tonight? She shudders at the thought and forces bad thoughts from her mind. "He has shown me nothing but kindness after bringing me here, I will trust him, for now," she says to herself. She can't shake her feelings, a mix of gratitude and fear toward him, unsure of the future.

13

After quite an extended period, the water in her bath begins to cool. She reluctantly stands up and takes the towel, drying and covering herself. She cautiously peeks out the door of the washroom to see if anyone is nearby. She knows I am the only other person in the house but remains cautious. She darts across the hall to the spare room and gets dressed in the clothes provided. She sits on the bed and takes a few minutes, warming in front of the fire, to process everything that has happened. Her mind thinks of her parents, and she prays that they are safe. She gets up and heads to the study.

As she enters the study she asks, "Well how do I look?" I look up and see her in the clothes I found. She is wearing brown, somewhat baggy pants, a white shirt, and a girls vest open in the front. The sleeves are rolled up, and she has a black belt around her waist to hold it all in place. Her long brown hair laying down across her shoulders. Her brown eyes sparkling. And she is smiling.

"You are stunning. It seems the clothes fit you okay. Are you comfortable?"

She comments, "thanks," and spins around. "They are a little baggy, but comfortable. Where did these come from and why do you have them here? Do you entertain many women who require a change of clothes?" she asks.

"Not at all. I am glad they fit you. As to their origin, that is a story for a different day. Please, sit down. How do you feel?" I offer her another glass of wine, and she happily accepts.

"So, have you been to this city before?" I ask.

"Never," she replies.

"Then you are not aware of the dangers that await us. This place is not what it once was. Violence and evil and corruption are everywhere."

"Alazaar," she exclaims.

I nod in agreement. "When we go out, it will be necessary for you to remain quiet. People will think of you as my slave and will not be kind. But you will be safe if you stay close to me. How long a trip is it to your village on foot?"

Gemma replies, "Probably five hours on foot. Are there no horses?"

"I have one, and we will take him, but slaves do not ride horses, and I will not ride while you walk."

Gemma nods, understanding. "I really want to return to my village and find my parents I will do whatever you ask. I only hope it remains, and my people are still there."

I simply nod, not knowing what to say. "Is your room, okay? Will you need anything else tonight? I ask her.

"The room is amazing, and very different from the wet ground or that cramped cage. Even in Timbervale we did not have such comfort. Our tiny home provided shelter and warmth, and we were happy and cared for, but we had no way to bathe inside, and our bed was a cot. I can never say thank you enough, and no, I do not require anything else."

"Very well then. We should conclude our day. My room is just down the hall if you need anything. Today has been eventful for sure, but I am glad I bought you Ms. Gemma. I believe I can help you, and it will be good for me to step into a new adventure. Even if only for a few days."

"I am glad you bought me too sir," she smiles slightly.

I respond, "Oh, do please stop calling me sir. My name is James."

She extends her hand to shake. I accept her hand as she exclaims, "Very nice to meet you, James." We shake hands.

15

Her hands are soft, tender, and small. But I feel a sense of pleasure just feeling her hand. We walk back to the bedrooms, blowing out candles along the way.

"Goodnight Gemma."

"Goodnight James."

The Journey Begins

I wake up early. The sun is just barely rising over the horizon, but the sky is blue, and I can see the castle and marketplace in the distance. I don't know what today will bring as we head to Gemma's village, but I fear the worst. Recent events in the kingdom have opened the door to lawlessness and violence. Our Kingdom is not the biggest, but we have always had good relations with our neighbors, and our people have been safe. Gemma's village is the first of such an attack that I've heard of, but if there's one, I'm sure there are others.

I fix up a small breakfast. Still no sign of Gemma, which isn't surprising given how exhausted she was. I go and knock on her door. "Gemma, are you awake?"

She replies, "Yes, come in." I open the door and step inside. Gemma is sitting up in bed, looking a bit tired still, but determined. "Good morning," she says.

"Good morning. Breakfast is in the kitchen, come down whenever you are ready. I had time to think last night after retiring. I want to talk with you over breakfast please."

Gemma smiles, "Breakfast sounds wonderful, thank you. I'll be right there, just give me a minute to freshen up please."

I nod and head back to the kitchen. Gemma quickly gets out of bed and heads to the washroom to brush her hair and freshen up. A few minutes later she makes her way to the kitchen.

Gemma comes and stands in the doorway looking around. The sunlight makes the whole house look different than the night before. It's nowhere near as dark and dreary as it seemed last night. It's actually pleasant. And the smell of breakfast fills the whole house.

"Bacon and fried eggs are on the stove. And there's fresh milk in the ice chest." I point to everything when I see her.

Her eyes widen at the sight of the delicious breakfast. Other than dinner last night, she hasn't had a proper meal in ages, and now breakfast this morning as well, she wonders again, who is this man. The smell of bacon and eggs makes her stomach growl. "Thank you, you are very kind, James," she says as she sits down at the table and begins to eat.

"Did you sleep well?" she asks.

"Yes, I slept very well, thank you. And you?"

"I slept wonderfully. I have never slept in a more comfortable bed."

We begin to eat, and I start to explain. "As I thought about everything last night, there is no need for us to delay in finding your parents. If you are up to it and believe you can travel, we can leave today. Right after eating. Staying here will only prolong the agony and risk one of us being seen in town, possibly starting an issue where one need not be. Forgive me for waking you up early, but it will be better if we leave early to Timbervale given it is such a long journey on foot."

Gemma eyes widen. "Oh yes sir, I can travel. I feel wonderful after that bath and such a good night sleep. I am ready immediately."

"Please eat your breakfast. We are not in that big a rush. I'm sure you are still a little weak from your time in captivity."

I set a collar and leash on the table. Her eyes show the terror. I explain to her: "When we leave, I must put this on you to protect you. People know me, and know I live alone. Plus, others would have seen me purchase you yesterday. The law now stipulates all slaves in transport will be collar-ed and shackled. If we are seen by Alazaar's men, and you are not bound, you could be severely beaten, and I could be put in jail as a criminal. Again, it is not my intent to hurt you. I promise I have never owned a slave, and I hate doing this, but it is only temporary and for a short distance."

Gemma's eyes fill with fear as she looks at the collar and leash. She swallows hard, her hands trembling. "I... I understand, but I'm scared...I don't want to wear that. It's just so degrading..."

I sit beside her and take her hand. "Would you rather be beaten if seen in public without it? I can't protect you from a mob, and it only takes one individual that recognizes me to start something. I promise you as soon as we are clear of the city I will remove it."

Gemma's face pales at the thought of being beaten. She knows I'm right and the fear of punishment outweighs her fear of discomfort from the collar. "No... I don't want to risk being beaten and would not want to jeopardize you after you've been so kind. I'll wear the collar but please be gentle with me."

She finishes eating, knowing she must trust me if she is to find her parents. But, she also realizes she has no reason to believe I would betray her. She has been comfortable all night and James paid a lot of money for her. After we cleanup she turns and looks at me. "You really promise to

18

remove it once clear of the city?"

"Yes, I promise! I understand your fear of me. I hope in time I can convince you I am sincere and earn your trust. I mean you no harm Gemma."

We clean up the kitchen and Gemma is smiling and happy, her eyes full of life. A far cry from the girl I picked out of a cage the day before.

"Are you ready?" I ask. I attach the collar to her neck and hand her the leash. "I don't like this either. I am terribly sorry, but it must be this way for now."

Gemma flinches slightly as I attach the collar to her neck, feeling the cold steel against her skin. She takes a deep breath, trying to steady herself. "It's okay. I know you're doing this to protect me. I just hate feeling like property."

"Well, you are not property." I hand her the key. "You keep this. If anything happens to me, you're too free yourself and run. Run fast and far."

"If something happens to you?" Gemma is frightened but takes a bit of comfort knowing she has the key to her freedom if needed. She takes a deep breath.... "I'm ready, and no matter what happens today, I shall never forget your kindness," she says.

"Hum, James. Will we need food for the journey? I can go without, you have already given me so much, but I do not want to see you hungry, and like you said, it is a long journey."

"That's an excellent idea, and something of which I hadn't thought. It has been so long since I've traveled anywhere. We will absolutely take food for you as well. You will never go hungry with me; I can promise that." With Gemma's help we gather additional supplies for the trip.

19

We head out to the stable to get the horse and begin our journey. I walk with Gemma rather than riding while she walks as I told her I would. I have the leash to her collar and to the horse in my hand and guide us down the property to the main street. But she still has the key. She points the way to her village – southeast it is. Gemma walks slightly behind me, her head down so as not to attract any attention. She knows once in the forest and away from the populace, she can relax.

We must pass through the busy markets. We dodge and weave around people, horses, wagons, and carts as vendors set up their goods for the day. The market is always a busy place with booths, food, people yelling, ugly buildings, and trash on the streets. Thieves and drunks are everywhere.

I keep an eye on Gemma, and she stays aware of our surroundings. I hear in the distance someone calling my name. "James. James, wait"

I stop to see Ivan approaching, waving, and smiling. Ivan is a friend about my age. We studied together when we were younger, and he is someone I can trust. Although I'd rather not engage in a social conversation at this time.

Ivan catches up with us. "James, my friend, it's good to see you out. I've feared the worst for you with everything going on. "He hugs me like a brother. As he releases me, he realizes I am holding a leash to both the horse and to Gemma. "James, what have we here? You have a slave girl?"

Ivan knows I would never own a slave, so if I'm leading a young woman around something is up. "She's beautiful James. Where did you get her?"

I look at Ivan. "This is Gemma. Gemma my friend Ivan." Gemma glances at Ivan. "Nice to meet you, Ivan." Ivan looks at me and makes a facial expression indicating 'what the hell?' without having to say anything aloud. I don't say anything at first. Then, "this isn't really a good time my friend. I needed a slave and bought one. We are embarking on a business trip and hope to return in a few days. Perhaps we can share a pint upon my return?"

Ivan knows everything I just said is a total lie, but he also knows to play along. "Well, you bought a fine girl my friend. and absolutely we shall share a pint upon your return. I look forward to hearing what has been happening." He hugs me again and whispers in my ear, "May the Gods bless you my friend, let me know if I can help with what you're up too." He winks at Gemma, "Take good care of him," he says to Gemma.

She nods.

We proceed on our way, hoping for no more delays. Once clear of the crowds Gemma whispers, "so Ivan is trustworthy?"

"Yes, I would trust Ivan with my life. He knew I was lying back there and played along anyway. And he knows I would never own a slave, so I am grateful for his support. Spies are everywhere, and one never knows who is listening."

Gemma smiles feeling some relief that I have good and dependable friends. We hurry through the rest of the market without incident. Once on the other side, it's not much further to the forest. We stay to the side of the road and make good time.

Within a half hour we are far enough away from the city that we can relax, and Gemma can remove her constraints. We stop and I assist her with her freedom. She moans as I free her hands and unlock the collar. She pulls it off fiercely and throws it on the ground. "Never again," she exclaims.

We still have a good four hour walk ahead of us, so we set out again. She begins to tell me more about Timbervale, her friends, her parents, and the good times she has had. And how excited she is to get back. There were three teenage girls that she was particularly fond of. The three had played together since they were young children and shared everything. She can't wait to see them again and tell them what happened to her.

After an hour we stop for another break. The forest is dense, the temperature is cool, and there is blue sky above the tall trees. "How can you stand living in the city with all this beautiful forest just begging to be explored?" she asks. She turns to me, and continues... "So where did the clothes I'm wearing come from? How is it you had women's clothing in your home? I have told you about me but know nothing of you."

"The clothes belonged to my wife."

"Your wife? You're married? Where is your wife?"

I pause. "My wife and 3-year-old daughter were killed. Murdered. Several months ago. Since then, you are really the first person I've interacted with."

Gemma freezes in her tracks. "Your family was killed? I'm so sorry. How terrible. How? By whom? Never mind, you don't have to talk about it. Wow, I feel so ...." She's unable to find the words to continue.

"She was only twenty-two years of age. She and my daughter were slaughtered during a riot by Alazaar's men. They were at the market when it came under attack. At least their deaths were quick, and they didn't suffer. Those are her clothes. I'm sorry, but it was all I had of her. I just couldn't bring myself to get rid of them."

Gemma gasps realizing she is wearing my deceased wife's clothes. "You shared your wife's clothing with me? I am honored that you shared them with me. I am so deeply sorry for what you must have gone through. Maybe are still going through."

"You remind me of her. Perhaps that is why I was so drawn to buy you yesterday. It's as if she was by my side telling me to do so. I think you two could have been friends."

"I wish I could have met her," she replies.

"Well, let us continue our journey." I feed and water the horse and we begin walking again. Soon we are stopped by the sound of approaching horses. "Gemma, hide in those bushes and stay quiet. No matter what happens, don't come out, understand." Gemma's fear comes back in full force, but she quickly takes cover in the brush knowing what may happen. She can see me, yet she's out of sight. I remain on the road with the horse as the men get close.

Five riders arrive and stop. The man in front says, "Who are you and what business have you out here? This is the land of Alazaar, and taxes must be paid to travel."

"I am James, of Artems, the capital city. I am a trader, bringing goods from the east and selling them in the market at Artems. I pay taxes to the authorities as required by law."

The front man turns to his companion. "Search his horse." The man jumps off his horse and makes his way to my saddle bags. He searches both and finds nothing but some food. He turns back to the leader and raises his arms empty.

"You travel light James of Artems. You have no bedroll, no extra provisions, and little food. Where are your goods?"

"I have sold them sir and am returning east to purchase more. I have friends along the way with whom I stay so have no need of a bed role."

The leader turns to his men. "Search the area. I do not trust this man." The men guide their horses around a large path looking for any sign that I am lying. All I can do is pray that Gemma is well enough hidden. After a few minutes they return to the leader. "There is no sign he is lying," says one of the men.

"Very well. You are free to go James but know this. I will look for you at the market next week. Pray I find you there before I find you back out here."

"Of course. I will be there." I reply to the leader. With that the men ride off. I offer the horse an apple hoping to stall until they are completely gone. Once they are far enough away, I call for Gemma, "Gemma are you there?" The brush rustles and Gemma appears. She runs back up to me.

"Are we safe?" she asks.

"I believe so. For now, anyway."

Gemma looks at me and says, "You told me the Kingdom was now dangerous, but I had no idea how dangerous. Thank you once more for protecting me."

"Yes, since Alazaar came to power, much has changed."

Gemma takes my hand, feeling safer doing so. "Timbervale is not much farther. I must let my people know everything I have learned." I enjoy the feeling of her hand in mine. It brings back good and happy memories.

Gemma's Village

Gemma talks once more about her excitement as we near Timbervale. She longs to hug her mother and father. We get close and she runs ahead, waving me on to walk faster. I pick up my pace and try to catch up with her.

Gemma tops the last hill, ready to see her friends and is instantly horrified. She stands there staring at what was once her village. She screams, and tears flow as she peers into the rubble. She falls to her knees hysterically and sobs.

What was once a vibrant community is now ash and dead bodies. Smoke rises from the smolders of what once were homes filled with love and laughter. The entire village – gone. I fall beside her and embrace her as she mourns on my shoulder. As she catches her breath, I take her hands in mine. I lift her face, so her eyes meet mine.

"We will figure this out, we will catch who did this." She wraps her arms around my neck.

"They're gone. It's all gone! My parents, my friends, my home. It's all gone!" Tears flood her eyes again. I sit there and just hold her, trying to offer some form of consolation.

After considerable time and lots of tears she looks at me and says, "We must look for survivors." She takes my hand. "Come on, let's go she says. There must be survivors."

We stand and begin to walk into what was once Timbervale, the smell of smoke and death is pungent. Nothing remains standing. We go from ash piles to ash piles looking for anyone still alive. Finally, we arrive at the spot that was her home. She kneels and weeps again. There is no sign of life anywhere. From the looks of things, with several fires still somewhat warm, this has all happened in just the last several days. We continue walking to the end of the road in her village.

She turns and looks back, tears flowing down her cheeks. "What will I do now?" she asks.

I reply, "Gemma, look at me, ... look at me." She turns and looks into my eyes. "Gemma something is not right. Yes, the buildings are gone. But I only counted six bodies. Wood fire does not burn bone; it doesn't get hot enough. The people are not here... The people are not here!"

Gemma turns and looks back at the ash. Then looks at me. She repeats, "The people are not here. Where are the people?" She asks herself out loud.

"They've either been captured or fled. You said there was over one hundred people here. It would take an army to capture a hundred people. No army did this. This is the work of marauders. The people fled. They had to have escaped. Where would they go? Think Gemma, where would they go?"

Gemma thinks a few moments, lost in thought, her eyes light up. "The Cave! They would have gone to the cave," she says.

Chapter TWO: New Hope

Gemma's People

"The cave? What cave? Do you know where it is? Do you know how to get there?" I ask.

Gemma grabs my arm. "Come on, let's go," she says.

We set out again, I know not where, but I follow her, leading the horse as we go.

"Please be there. Oh, please be there," she cries.

We walk for over an hour. Gemma stops.

"Leave the horse here, we must be quiet. If my people are not here, who knows if others are," says Gemma.

I tie the horse to a tree, and we continue walking; down between huge boulders, along a windy path, as we head down the steep hill.

Suddenly I hear a wheezing sound, and pain explodes in my shoulder. I collapse to the ground in agony. Blood flows from my left shoulder. Gemma gasps and comes to my aid. "James!" she screams as she comes to comfort me. "James, your shoulder! You've been hit with an arrow," she exclaims. Within minutes men are surrounding us, swords pointing at me, while others pull Gemma away from me.

"Stop!" she shouts. She recognizes the men. "He saved me. Do not hurt him, what have you done?" She breaks free and runs back to my side. She pulls back my shirt. "The arrow did not go through, and it's not deep," she explains. A man steps behind me, grabs the arrow, and rips it from my shoulder. I collapse into Gemma's arms from the pain.

"Lucky for you Rowan is a terrible shot," says some strange man. He holds out his hand offering to help me stand. I take his hand.

Another man steps forward, "Gemma, by God's grace... you're alive."

"Warren!" Gemma leaps into his arms. "We returned to Timbervale and found the ashes. I feared you all dead, but James forced me to think of where you would go. There were no bodies so we came here as fast as we could. Oh I prayed you all would be here."

She turns to me, but speaking to Warren she says, "Warren, this is James, he saved me from the slave traders." One by one the men step up and hug Gemma, welcoming her back.

Warren extends his hand to shake. "Thank you for rescuing our Gemma. Please forgive the arrow; seems Rowan got a little carried away. Come, we must head to safety, the woods are not safe anymore."

Gemma helps me as I walk, my shoulder hurting bad, blood running down my arm. She pushes my shirt against the wound to help stop the bleeding. We walk a short distance to the opening of a cave. People are gathered inside and out. A scream comes from the distance.

"Gemma!"

A middle-aged lady runs in our direction. She screams again "Gemma," tears flowing down her face. Gemma looks to see the woman.

"Mom!" Shouts Gemma running to greet her.

Tears flow as both women begin wailing. They leap into each other's arms. The woman lifts Gemma off the ground at their reunion, her arms firmly embracing her.

"Oh Gemma, I thought you were dead, or worse. Praise God you're alive and found your way back to us," says her mom. The two break their embrace and stare at each other.

"Oh Mom, I was so scared when we found the village destroyed. What happened? Where's dad?"

I make my way over to Gemma and her mom.

"Oh, mom, this is James." Gemma introduces me to her mom. "He's been injured, but he saved me."

Gemma's mom hugs me for saving Gemma, and I winch in pain as she does. "Oh goodness, forgive me." She jumps back seeing my reaction. "Come, let us get you bandaged. How can we ever repay you for bringing my Gemma back to us?" As we enter the cave another girl about Gemma's age runs up and hugs her. "Gemma, oh Gemma, you're alive and back. We were so worried about you and the others."

"Abbie!" cries Gemma. The girls hug, and cry, while embracing each other.

Gemma's mom says, "okay, there will be plenty of time to catch up later. Gemma, we must tend to James." Both girls help me move to a large table, and another lady comes over to treat my wound.

"That's a nasty wound," she says as she pours what must have been alcohol on it. Again, the pain explodes in my brain. Then she bandages it and bids me well. "That's going to hurt for a few days, but you'll be fine. Just don't be using that arm any more than you have too," she says.

"Thank you, and I won't," I reply.

Gemma says, "Thank you Clara, we'll make sure he's taken care of."

Gemma's mom sets a pint of beer in front of both Gemma and me. "We have beer or water; I thought you would enjoy a beer for your nerves. Welcome James, I'm Madeline, Gemma's mom, and I'm so happy to meet you. And Clara, the woman who bandaged your arm acts as our nurse. She keeps us all bandaged when we get hurt." Madeline laughs, jiggles, and expresses so much happiness I feel she may burst.

"Mom, where's dad? And all the others?" asks Gemma again.

Another man speaks up. "They've been taken." He sits at the table and shakes my hand. "Welcome, I am Orien. You've met Warren. Together we've worked to secure some safety for us. You're both very lucky to be alive. Warren and I act as Community leaders. There are others, men that form a steering committee for the community, but they've been taken. So, we're trying to hold our community together as best we can for now."

"I'm so sorry about what has happened to you all, and for your lost family members. We saw the bodies at Timbervale. Nice to meet you, Orien."

Gemma's mom speaks up. "Gemma, the morning you were taken, some twenty-armed men stormed the village. They rounded us all up like dogs, the ones they could anyway. Many of us ran into the forest, others were killed, a lot were taken. They had huge wagons with cages made of thick iron bars. Those that fought, died."

"Taken where, mom?" asks Gemma.

"Oh child, we wish we knew. Men and women both. We fear they may have been executed; we knew some would be sold. Of the one hundred and five of us, now only thirty-five remain. Thirty-seven with you two."

A woman comes to the table with food. "You must be starved. Hi, I'm Katherine. Things are bad, but we have food. Please, eat!"

Gemma and I both thank Katherine and take a piece of bread and some fruit to go with our beer.

Madeline continues, "Gemma, tell us what happened after you were taken. I saw a man pull you up onto his horse and that was it, you were gone."

The room falls silent as Gemma begins to explain. "The man on the horse grabbed me and held me by my hair, so I couldn't escape. We rode for maybe two hours west and came upon a house. He knew the man there, and I was given to another man to be sold as a slave. They put me in a cage and kept me prisoner for three days. Then I was being transported to the Westen Markets to be sold to the highest bidder, but we stopped in the city of Artems for some reason, I do not know why. While there, James saw me and bought me from the merchant. He paid six-hundred Lyra for me." The room gasps as Gemma explains the cost and her purchase.

Gemma continues to tell them of last evening. Coming to my home; being set free; fed an amazing dinner; how impressive the bath and bed were; and of our travels today – back to Timbervale, and finally the cave.

Everyone cheers when she finishes speaking. Gemma takes and squeezes my hand, smiling at me as she does so.

Gemma's mom begins to cry again.

Orien speaks. "James, what you have done is beyond common kindness. We cannot repay you, but we can accept you as one of us if you will stay."

"Of course he can stay," says Gemma. Then she looks at me, "You can stay, right?"

I don't answer.

Orien speaks again. "We believe the women, or at least some of the women have been taken to Artems to work, while others have been sold. And most of the men have more than likely been taken to the Twin Springs Mine as slave labor. The men you see here now were not in Timbervale when the marauders arrived. The woman who escaped knew to come here, to this cave. Everyone in Timbervale has always been taught to come here if disaster struck. We always assumed it would be from a fire. Not marauders. The ones that escaped that day all met up here by evening."

Warren speaks up. "It is our desire to rescue our people, but we are few in number, against trained and well-equipped soldiers. Do you have connections in the city with anyone who can help us?"

"I may be able to help, but I was not prepared for all of this. My plan was to return Gemma to her people, to her parents, and return to Artems. Much is happening there, and I am part of it. Our Kingdom has changed. Peace has been shattered."

A man from the back yells, "This is the fault of King Edmonds. He has betrayed us all. We will fight to our death to take back our Kingdom!"

"Here here," the crowd exclaims. Cheering at the man's words.

Warren speaks to me again. "What can you tell us of the city, of its people? We are far from the politics of the King and his rule. We have lived a peaceful life here until last week. What are the plans of our King? Please tell us anything you know."

The man in the back yells again. "His plan is to kill us all."

The crowd waits, waiting for me to answer. Gemma puts her hand on my shoulder. I pause and take a deep breath.

"Several months ago, our King was replaced by an evil man named Alazaar. Alazaar has a very strong Army. He pillages our land, rapes our women, and steals our resources. Even now he controls the Twin Springs Mine, selling our minerals and stones for his own glory."

Someone else speaks up, a woman, "I have heard of Alazaar. I heard he and the King are partners. They are working together to stomp out freedoms and to tax us all into poverty."

I stand up and look around the room. It's easy to see the fear and anger in everyone's eyes. I begin to explain, "Alazaar and the King were friends. The intent of the partnership was to make the Kingdom better; safer. Alazaar betrayed our King and exiled him."

The crowd murmurs. Someone yells, "death to King Edmonds. We don't believe you."

I wave my hand, "please, please, do not fault our King. The fault is not with him. He is a good and innocent man. After the loss of our Queen Maria, he was never the same. He trusted Alazaar."

"Liar! Why should we believe you?" says the man in the back. He continues, "over the last six months our markets have been raided, our villages destroyed, our women stolen from us. All under the watchful eye of King Edmonds. So again, why should we believe you?"

I pause and continue looking around the room. The faces of people in misery. Living in fear. My heart is moved. I look at Gemma. She also is frightened of everything that has happened. I see the concern in her eyes.

I pause for an extended period of time, then remark:

"Because he is my father."

The room falls silent.

Gemma gasps.

Orien speaks, "You are Prince James Edmonds?"

"I am."

"Alazaar betrayed my father and has him locked up in the dungeon of the castle. He murdered my wife and my young daughter. He has taken control of the Kingdom. And I am only allowed to live as his puppet."

Murmurs grow loud. Gemma is in shock. "Why didn't you tell me?"

I look at her, "Because, as I said, I expected to return you to your parents and return home. You would be safe, and I would have helped prevent another one of our beautiful women being carted off like a caged animal. I'm sorry. I never meant to deceive you, Gemma."

Gemma remains seated, thinking for a few moments. She then stands and comes by my side. Looking me in the eye she says, "Your Highness, I believe you, and I will stand by your side and fight with you to retake our Kingdom."

Madeline comes and curtsies in front of me. "Your Highness. I am with my daughter and with you. I can never repay you for what you have done for my Gemma, but I pledge my life in your service."

Other women follow Madeline's example. One-by-one they come up to the table, curtsy, and echo, "Your Highness."

Warren bows his head, "Your Highness, forgive us. We have been through much and had no idea who you are."

I grasp Warren by the forearm. "How could you have known? Do not apologize. I did not identify myself out of fear of placing you all in danger. If Alazaar discovers I have been here, who knows what he would do." I turn to Gemma, "I must go back. I hope you understand."

Gemma nods and lowers her head in sadness. She had hopes that I could and would help her people.

Orien speaks up again, "Your Highness, if you go back, what will you do? May we help you? We are not afraid of Alazaar, and we will fight by your side. If everything you have said is true, and I believe it is, we must find a way to retake our Kingdom."

He continues, "Very well, if you must return, but tonight stay with us. You cannot travel back in the dark."

"You are all very generous. To you in the back, so sure my father has betrayed our Kingdom, come with me, and I will show you he has not. I will stay tonight, thank you for your kindness."

Gemma and I continue eating the fruit and bread on the table. After eating I look to Gemma, "would you like to take a walk?"

Gemma smiles. "Absolutely Your Highness." She takes my hand, and we walk outside, again feeling some security and safe with me in light of the last day and knowing I am the Prince. There's a crowd outside the cave, and a few campfires already burning. As we walk past people, they look at us and whisper amongst themselves. Those close enough to speak clearly to us acknowledge us.... "Your Highness; Gemma." Their greeting seems strange. No one has greeted me by my title since I was exiled after my wife died.

Gemma leads me down by a small river and sits up on a rock overlooking the area. "What's it like being a Prince, Your Highness?" She looks at me, then blushing she looks away. She continues, "I'm ashamed and embarrassed I didn't know you were the Prince. Please forgive me."

"Gemma, there is nothing to forgive. I intentionally did not identify myself to you, and besides, no one in the cave recognized me either. I guess I should be embarrassed that I don't act 'princely'."

"Being a Prince is different I suppose. I never worried about what I would eat, or where I would sleep. I've never bathed in a river or went without a coat. Being out amongst our people has been enlightening. I have always been kept from our people, for fear of my safety. I'm glad that I now have a chance to meet the people we rule. Or did rule."

"You are correct that no one recognized you. We have been secluded from the activities of the Kingdom which probably made us easy prey for those marauders. It's good that you have seen the struggles of the people. Someday when you are King, you can help ease their burdens."

"When I am King? I have no army to defeat Alazaar. Most people don't even recognize me even in the city. I fear I shall never be King. Buying you was the biggest thing I've done in months. I'm happy I've done it, but what now?"

Gemma jumps off the rock and comes to me. "What now? You are our leader. My people will follow you; I know they will. You can't give in to despair or there is no hope for any of us. You must help us Your Highness."

"I would love to help you, but what can I do? I have no military training; I have had swordsmanship lessons, but no weapons for an army, I am one man, exiled into dust."

"Forgive me Your Highness, but you can't think like that. Our Kingdom depends on you now. Men will follow you. My leaders will follow you if you ask them."

"Follow me where? I've got a handful of men in the city who are loyal. We've been watching, listening, thinking of a way, hoping for an opportunity."

I stop speaking, my mind spinning with thoughts. I grab Gemma's hand and start back to the cave. "I'm an idiot. Come with me. You are right Gemma, why did I not see it? This IS the opportunity; we must talk to Orien and Warren. Come."

I turn to return to the Cave, but Gemma stops me. "Your Highness, what are you talking about? What opportunity?" she asks.

I smile, almost giddy. "Gemma. First, please stop calling me Your Highness. You've called me James since we met. At least when it's just us, please. I appreciate your respect for who I am, but right now I need you as a confidant and a friend. Not as a loyal subject. I trust you. I need you. Now come with me I know what to do."

I practically drag Gemma as I hurry us back. We head to the meeting table in the cave. Orien and Warren are both there. "Perfect. You're both here. How many women were taken?" I ask.

Orien replies, "Twenty-Nine Your Highness. Why?"

"Because I'm pretty sure I know where they are, and we're going to rescue them."

Gemma grabs my arm, "You know where they are?"

Orien adds, "We can rescue them? How? Tell us everything you are thinking."

The people around the cave close in, and the people listening outside step inside, all excited to hear my thoughts. Gemma gasps, putting her hands over her mouth.

A lady I do not know steps forward, "You Highness, you know where are daughters are? You can rescue them?" Tears stream down her face.

I continue, "I can't promise anything, and I'll need people who will recognize your women. But make no mistake, this will be dangerous.

Gemma shouts first, "I'm coming with you."

Orien says, "Me too. I'll go."

Two other women step forward. "Two of them are our daughters, we'll go." Gemma hugs the ladies and turns to me, "Your Highness, this is Camilla and Nadia." Both women curtsy and smile.

Warren speaks, "Orien we can't leave the camp defenseless. I should remain here, although I long to come with you and help."

"Warren, remaining here will take much worry off us and be a huge help. Your time to fight will come. Please, protect those remaining here. I Thank you." We lock forearms, and nod at each other.

"Okay, I will bet my own head that the women were taken to the brothels to work - as Orien suggested earlier. And yes, Orien, the men absolutely would have been taken to the Mine as slave labor. Right now, we can't help the men, that's a different fight, but we can get the women. I think."

"Now, the brothels. There are two such places in the city."

Several women gasp and begin to cry.

Camilla echoes my words, "The brothels, are you sure? Our daughters!" She places her hands on her cheeks.

I try to calm everyone. "Forgive my vulgar language, but now is not the time to be timid. We must understand what we are up against. I have never visited such places, but I have heard stories. First and most importantly, if the women are there, they are alive. Second, they are treated well. The house owners expect profit, and that doesn't come from injured or sick girls. Lastly, new girls function as servants until they are chosen for work. It's been less than a week, I believe all of them would still be untouched."

Gemma speaks up "Our Prince is right, and we must trust him and keep our hope alive. Our daughters and sisters and neighbors deserve at least that."

The crowd claps and cheers at Gemma's words.

Orien asks, "What's the plan?"

I turn back to Gemma, "Gemma, you've been through a lot. Are you sure you're up for this? No one would think less of you for staying here."

Gemma doesn't even blink before answering. "I'm going with you," she says staring at me.

Madeline speaks up, "Gemma, are you sure? I can't bear to lose you again."

Gemma retorts, "I'm going mother. I must go. Those girls are my friends." She hugs her mother and follows up by saying "I'll be fine."

She looks back at me, "The plan?"

"Okay, there are two such houses in the city." I bend down and draw a map in the dirt. "Gemma, Camilla, and I will take one house. Orien, Nadia, and friends I have in the city will take the other - tomorrow night, after dark. Gemma, you and I will return early in the day tomorrow and connect with my friends. Orien, Camilla, and Nadia, I want you to leave later. Much later, so that you arrive at my house after dark." I show them in the dirt the path to take to arrive at the back of my house. "There is much less risk of being seen this way."

"My house is always watched by Alazaar's men. Gemma, they would have seen you with me already, thinking you to be my slave. You can come with me. In fact, it will cause suspicion if you are not with me, but it will mean wearing the collar again, briefly."

Gemma nods, "I can do that if it means getting our women back," she responds.

We go over in detail the planned events to get the women. "Anyone and everyone who has questions is free to ask them."

"Horses and wagons." I think out loud. "We need a way to transport all the women back here. Who has wagons that can meet us at the Lakehouse to transport all the women back here?"

Two women in the group yell, "We don't know where the Lakehouse is, but we can do that, we have wagons and horses and can fix them up to bring everyone back. We'd love to help Your Highness."

"Perfect. May I ask your names? I would like to know all of you, please."

"Yes, Your Highness. I'm Amelia."

"And I'm Luna, Your Highness."

"Very nice to meet both of you. Thank you for volunteering." A few questions are raised and clarified, but within the hour we have a solid plan. Katherine brings us all another beer and we toast to success.

Gemma raises her pint of beer, "A toast to our Prince, who God has sent back to us."

I feel embarrassed but join in the fun. After a while Gemma and I walk back outside into the night air. It's chilly but there is an excitement in the air. "You have brought hope to my community." Gemma smiles big, the first time she has done so since we met. Her smile warms my heart.

"So, James, are you ready for this?" she asks.

"Oh, I am so ready. You were right. I had fallen into despair. I could not see a way to fight back until you said what you said. Suddenly it just came to me, like a vision. It became clear of what we must do. Thank you for all the courage you've shown. You could have easily run-away last night, but you chose to stay."

Gemma smiles. "You're a good man James. I can tell, and I trust you. Soon everyone will trust you."

"Thank you, Gemma. Thank you for your encouragement. You know, you've turned out to be quite a bargain for only six hundred Lyras." I laugh aloud and so does Gemma. "Come on," she says, "my mom has prepared a cot for you to sleep on, close to us. It's very different from the beds in your home, but hopefully it will be acceptable."

"It will be fine." She takes my hand and leads me. It is late, and we need sleep. She walks me to my cot. "Here is yours. My mother and I are right over there. Good night, Your Highness." She curtsy's grinning, having never curtsied to a Prince before, feeling a little awkward.

"Good night, Gemma. Sleep well."

Danger Awaits

I wake up early, my shoulder in pain from the arrow the night prior. I look around, most people are still asleep, including Gemma and her mom. So, I make my way to the meeting table in the larger area of the cave. Katherine is up humming a song and fixing food.

"Good morning, Katherine."

She looks up, "Oh good morning Your Highness. Would you like a cup of coffee, and did you sleep well? she asks.

"I'd love a cup of coffee, and I slept okay. What are you doing awake so early?

She waves her hand at me. "I'm not one to sleep the day away, early to rise, early to bed, makes us healthy, wealthy, and wise they say, or something to that affect." She chuckles and pours me a cup of coffee.

"Is that so? And how's that working out for you?" I ask grinning.

She laughs loudly, "Well now, that's a better conversation had over a pint rather than morning coffee. Come back tonight and I'll let you know." She laughs and returns to making food for folks.

I sip my coffee, thinking about the day ahead, or rather, the rescue operation planned for today. A million thoughts of failure race through my mind. I shake them away and force myself to think positively. These are good people, and we have exceptionally good chances of victory.

A few people wake up and come strolling in also seeking coffee. They acknowledge my presence but don't speak much. Soon I hear Gemma walking in, greeting others as she passes them.

"Good morning Your Highness, how are you feeling?" she asks.

"My shoulder is letting me know it's there, but I'm okay. The coffee is good. How do you have coffee?"

Gemma answers, "We traded lumber for what we need, but I don't know what we will do in the future. Timbervale was our home and our business." She frowns and looks sad.

"Hey, you'll rebuild. We're going to get your people back. All of them. Then rebuild. The forest isn't going anywhere, trees will always supply lumber." I try to encourage her. Especially after the pep talk, she gave me last night.

She squeezes my hand and says, "Thanks James."

I smile and she gets coffee as well. She greets the others, knowing all of them by name. She hugs some, others she just chats with and passes on a smile. It is becoming obvious she is a natural leader and helps hold this community together. She's wearing different clothes today. Some of her own I suppose. I wonder if that yellow dress was salvageable. She returns to where I'm sitting and refills my coffee.

She asks, "So when do we leave? It won't take as long today; I'll have my horse."

"That's wonderful, and it will certainly make the trip easier. Just remember, slaves don't ride horses." I wink at her and chuckle.

"I know, I know, and I'll have to wear that stupid collar, but we can ride most of the way." She shrugs her shoulders and drinks her coffee.

Before long Orien and others arrive as well. This table serves as kind of a community hall, and town square combined. Gemma again acknowledges all of them.

"You ready for this today, Orien?" I ask.

"Yes, Your Highness," he replies. "We are excited to get our woman back and begin to rebuild. We will arrive at your home tonight after dark. Everything is set."

"Sounds good, today we start taking back our Kingdom." I reply.

"We're all ready to follow you," says Gemma.

We eat some breakfast and ready the horses for the return trip. I second guess myself regarding the details of the plan and worry about placing Gemma in danger, but I know Gemma would never stay here, and I have faith in Orien's ability to lead a group.

A few minutes later Camilla and Nadia come in. Camilla speaks, "our horses are ready, as is the wagon to bring our women home. Amelia and Luna did a great job adding hay to the wagon and adding some side rails to protect anyone from falling off. We will have it staged at the Lakehouse just like we planned."

"That's good Camilla, thank you both for joining us today." I say in reply.

The Lakehouse is about thirty minutes from the city. It's more a barn than a house, along the edge of a large lake. It's not far out of the way between Artems and the cave, and it will provide shelter and a place to regroup as needed after we rescue the women. It will also provide a place to prepare for the trip back to the cave in the dark. It will be dangerous traveling at night, but we have no choice.

A short while later, Gemma and I are ready. Madeline hugs Gemma and begins to cry. "Oh Gemma, I'm so proud of you. You're so brave, but I still worry about your safety. Please be careful." Madeline looks to me, "you will take care of her Your Highness, please? I can't lose her again."

Gemma holds her mom tight, "I'll be fine mom, and I will return."

To put her mom at ease I remark, "Madeline, the probability exists that she will take better care of me than I her, but I also believe we will be fine. No one expects that we would dare make a rescue attempt, so we will have the element of surprise."

Madeline nods and helps Gemma mount her horse. Orien bids us well and we depart.

The Journey Home

The horses are a pleasant addition for the return trip. It is an exceptionally long walk. Plus, they will make for a fast escape should the need arise. We travel for around half an hour and Gemma hasn't said a word. So, I ask … "Are you okay Gemma? You haven't said a word since we left. Are you still good with the plan?"

She looks over at me. "Forgive me James. I'm still processing everything that has happened. In eight days, I've gone from being a simple village girl, to a slave, to freedom, to embarking on a daring adventure with the Prince of our Kingdom, to rescuing women that were kidnapped! It's a little overwhelming and I've not thought through it all."

"I suppose you're right. It would be a lot for experienced adults. To say nothing of a young yet brave girl. You've done amazingly well through all of it, and I believe in you. I'm glad you're here. I fear most young girls would have died in that slaver's cage. You're a strong woman Gemma."

Gemma blushes as I compliment her. "I'm not sure I'd be so strong had it not been for your rescue Your Highness," she replies.

We continue, enjoying the beauty of the day, and the quiet of the woods. Most trade and commerce are accomplished via the northern routes, and Timbervale and the cave being to the southeast leave little traffic to contend with. We stop after a couple of hours to eat and give the horses some rest.

We talk about tonight's plans and what to do if things go wrong. Escaping back to the Lakehouse is the first plan. "If we are captured, any women that are freed are to be taken to the cave immediately. No one is to wait or attempt a rescue of anyone on the team. We will have to improvise. If I am captured, Alazaar would dare not put me to death for fear of causing an uprising among the people."

Gemma concurs as we walk around a bit, stretching our legs after the time on the horse. We eat some fruit and lead the horses to water in a nearby stream. After a brief period, we mount up and head northwest once more. Next stop, the Lakehouse.

We near the Lakehouse and see horses. If soldiers are there tonight it will ruin our plans, endangering all of us. I worry they may be part of the same five men we encountered on our trip yesterday, but there are only two horses. We stop far from the Lakehouse and just watch. After about an hour we see people walking out to the horses.

It's two women. I recognize one of them. "Jump on your horse, let's catch them before they leave." We both jump on the horses and ride fast to the Lakehouse. The visitors notice us ride up and draw swords. As I get close, one of the girls yells my title, "Your Highness." She sheaths her sword and runs to greet me. I dismount, and help Gemma do the same. I turn as the woman wraps her arms around me. "Your Highness, I can't believe you're here. I thought you were dead."

"Sarah!" I return her embrace. "What are you doing here? It's so wonderful to see you." I turn to Gemma, "Gemma, meet Princess Sarah of Westerly. Sarah, this is Gemma." Sarah embraces Gemma informally. "Pleasure to meet you," she says.

Gemma returns the gesture. "Princess," she remarks, partly being respectful, partly being quizzical.

Princess Sarah turns and introduces her companion, "This is Alexandra, my security and best friend." Sarah introduces us and we nod.

"Come let us go inside, we have much to catch up on," I say.

We enter the Lakehouse and Gemma gets drinks from our saddle bags. Sarah begins, "Oh James, tell me everything. I thought you had been executed months ago. It is so wonderful to see you alive. What about your father, is he still alive?"

My reply to that is simply, "Sarah, what are you doing here of all places?"

"We are returning to Westerly," she replies. "We came to Artems last week. Hearing rumors of the violence and villages that have fallen under attack in your Kingdom. We needed to know what has happened, but our search for answers only provided us with despair, and no answers. I was returning to tell my father the news, and to expect that Westerly was at risk of invasion."

"Yes, Gemma's village was attacked and destroyed." I explain everything that has happened. About my family, my father, and Alazaar. About Gemma and her people, and how we are returning to rescue the women. "Join us." I remark. "We could use your help, and certainly the help of Alexandra. We have few people with training in how to fight."

Sarah looks to Alexandra and asks, "What do you think, are you up for a fight?"

"Always my lady. Especially to help others who obviously are so dear and in need."

Sarah turns back to me, "Well, Your Highness, count us in. We'll get those women." She then speaks to Gemma, "and you, Gemma, such a beautiful young girl. Are ready to learn to fight and help take back your Kingdom?"

Gemma replies, "Absolutely Princess. From the moment that man pulled me on his horse I was ready to fight. And since James rescued me, it seems I will get my chance. I'm glad that you're willing to join us. I want our women, and men, back with us."

"James?" Sarah asks quizzically at the informal reference using only my name, a huge smile on her face. She knows for me to allow that, there is a connection between Gemma and me. I put her concerns to rest. "Sarah, after Amira and Destiny were murdered, my father imprisoned, and I exiled from the castle, no one has referred to me as Prince until I arrived at the Cave. And as to my father, yes, I believe he is still alive. In Alazaar's dungeon. I fear for him."

Sarah responds, "Oh James, we had no idea. My father would have sent an army to have helped King Edmonds. My father has always been friends with and respected your father. But we're here now, and we will not abandon you. After your women are freed, I will return to my Kingdom and inform my father of everything that has happened."

I explain to Sarah about the Cave and the journey we're embarking on. Then facing her, I take hold of her hands. "Thank you. Help us tonight, then yes, tomorrow you must ride to your father and explain everything. Tonight, we will get the women, and I have hope of rescuing the men in the coming weeks, but we will need your army, and the armies of the south to defeat Alazaar, and make all our lands safe once again."

Sarah embraces me once more, saying, "Then let us all be on our way."

Gemma remarks, "collar time for me," she says begrudgingly.

"Oh yes, I completely forgot, thank you for saying something." I get the collar and suggest to Sarah, "Sarah, it would be best for you and Alexandra to ride ahead. We will meet you in the tavern on the north side of the market. There we will connect with my friend Mark, and then we can throw this collar away Gemma."

"Praise the gods," she quips back.

"Nonsense James. We will ride with you and fight with you, if necessary," says Sarah.

"Very well. I welcome your company." We mount up and ride to Artems. On the way I explain the plan to rescue the women. Gemma and Alexandra talk about their homes and seem to become friends. Although Alexendra looks to be maybe twenty-eight or twenty-nine years old, so she's much older than Gemma. And Sarah is thirty-one, I have complete confidence in her judgement and experience. Alexandra and Sarah are both built like warriors, with strong arms, strong shoulders, and strong legs. Both women are wearing light clothing and full armor.

As we get closer to the city, Gemma and I once again set out on foot, to keep from drawing any attention to ourselves. Sarah and Alexandra move ahead but remain in sight. As we arrive at the market a man stops us.

"How much for your slave girl," he asks.

"She is not for sale," I state firmly.

"All slaves are for sale, how much for the girl?" he retorts.

In the next second there is knife blade at the man's throat. "The girl is not for sale." Alexandra remarks, while holding the knife ready to send the man to his grave. The man raises his arms in the air. "Not for sale, yes, yes, not for sale. I understand," the would-be buyer fearfully remarks.

"Now get out of here," says Alexandra. The man quickly runs away. The incident has drawn some attention, so we hurry to the Tavern to meet Mark.

As we enter, I hear Mark, "My good friend James, how wonderful you are here." He comes over too us and introductions are made. He notices the collar on Gemma. "A slave girl? James. I know better. Come let us all go upstairs where we may drink and talk in private."

The upper room is small but has a table big enough for all of us to sit. I remove the collar from Gemma and hand it to Mark. "Here, sell this thing Mark; we have no need of it anymore." Mark nods and throws the collar and shackles on a side table. Gemma smiles knowing that humiliation is over. We sit down and pints of beer are brought to us. I then explain everything going on to Mark and ask his help to rescue the women tonight.

"Of course we'll assist you, James. I can tell you; your women are there. We saw a cage full of women arrive in town several days ago, not knowing from where they had come.

Gemma gasps at hearing the news. "They're alive?" she begs to know.

"Well, I can't promise they're your group of women, but I know new women were brought in. Young and middle-aged women. Taken to both evening houses. Do not worry about them, they have been well taken care of there."

Gemma remarks looking at me. "That's not very reassuring, but it has to be them. We've heard nothing of any other villages being raided in the last two weeks."

Mark offers us food as it's getting late, and we all happily accept his hospitality.

"Thank you, my friend. I will see to it you are paid for all this."

Mark laughs. "You bet your ass I'll be paid, and then some." He jokes with me, knowing that I pay my debts, and that I am in his debt for helping us.

Food is provided and everyone gets to know everyone. Mark introduces two more of his friends, Ivan and Luis.

"James, you're back," says Ivan.

"Ivan, it's good to see you again my friend. Thank you for your help in the market the other day. You've met Gemma, and she is no slave. It's a long story."

"And one I look forward to hearing soon," he replies.

"You two know each other, that's helpful," says Mark.

So, we now have a good supply of help for two groups. One for each house simultaneously. We share the plan with the two men. After a couple of hours, the sun is down so we can move more freely back to my home and await the arrival of Orien, Camilla, and Nadia from the cave.

Chapter THREE: Saving the Women

The First House

We arrive at my home and tend to the horses, then go in and start a fire. Sarah remarks, "Wow James, this very different from the castle, but it is comfortable. Your home, however, is in the castle, and we are going to get you back there."

"Thank you, Sarah. All in its proper time, all in the proper time."

A short while later we hear tapping at the back entrance. Sure enough, Orien, Camilla, and Nadia make their way inside. Gemma hugs Orien and the ladies and asks about their trip.

"The trip was good, how was yours," Orien asks.

We introduce Princess Sarah and Alexandra, as well as Mark, Luis and Ivan to Orien, Camilia, and Nadia. "Ten of us, five per team, that's perfect." I remark.

Camilia and Nadia both know the girls that were taken, so we assign one to each group.

The First House team then is Gemma, Sarah, Alexandra, Nadia, and me. That leaves Orien, Mark, Luis, Camilia, and Ivan for the second house. We double check all our supplies and head out under the cover of night.

We travel the back roads to the houses and arrive with no incident. They are only a couple blocks apart, and the women are often shared between the two. The two groups separate and head to their assigned house. My group takes the first house. It is filled with people, with several guards in the front and in the back. The house is large with two floors and several rooms on each floor, in addition to a kitchen and a large gathering area.

Sarah quips, "Going in through the front is out of the question."

Alexandra motions she's going to check out the far side.

The rest of us move to the back of the house. It's less crowded, but there are still several people and a couple of guards. The left side of the house is well lit, ruling out any possibility of entrance there. That leaves crossing roof tops and the second floor, or...

Alexandra returns, "follow me" she says.

We follow her around to the north side of the house. It's much darker and she points to a room on the first floor with no lights on. There's no one in sight over here, so we make our way to the window of the dark room. Sarah and Alexandra keep watch while we peer in. It seems empty. The window is locked, but Nadia has it open in seconds with a knife she carries. She looks inside and whispers back, "it's empty."

I assist Nadia, and then Gemma, helping them to get inside, followed by Sarah. Alexandra motions for me to go next and I oblige her since she has the sword. I climb in and then Alexandra follows me without issue.

Gemma looks at me. "Now what?"

Before I can answer Nadia opens the door quietly and peers down the hall. The hall is empty, but she sees people in the parlor area, drinking and laughing. As she watches through the narrow slit, she gasps. She closes the door and turns to us.

"I saw Irene! she whispers emphatically. That means some of them are here."

We all quietly make hand gestures expressing in silence our joy that one of the community members has been spotted, trying hard not to make any noise.

"She was serving drinks."

"I have an idea," Nadia adds.

Nadia quickly grabs a robe hanging by the bed and a wig laying on the dresser. She throws it on, and quietly slips out the door into the hall. The rest of us object quietly, but it happens so fast, all we can do now is wait and hope.

Nadia walks down the hall with confidence hoping to catch Irene, but Irene is too fast and heads back to the kitchen. As Nadia steps into the parlor and begins making her way to the door on the other side, she is stopped by a man holding a drink.

"Good evening my dear," he says. "Please allow me to introduce myself. I am Thomas, and you are?"

Nadia is a beautiful woman with long blond hair and brown eyes in her mid-thirties. She accepts the man's invitation to talk so as to blend in. "Good evening fine sir, are you having a good time tonight?" She slides her arm around the man's back and gets really close.

"I'm doing much better now. Where have you been hiding? I don't recall having ever seen you here before. Are you new?" he asks.

"Oh, I've been bathing and making myself pretty for you gentlemen tonight. And yes, I came in this past week at the request of friends I have here in Artems. Are you from here Thomas?"

"I am indeed, and it is so wonderful that you have joined us." He turns to introduce her to others. In that moment Nadia knocks his drink from his hand, spilling it on the floor.

"Oh, my heavens, look what I have done. Please forgive me Thomas, I shall quickly fetch you another."

Thomas jumps as his drink spills over him and onto the floor. "Don't worry my dear, accidents do happen. But yes, I'm afraid now I'm quite a mess. Would you please fetch me another while I go clean up." Thomas heads to the washroom, while Nadia makes her way to the kitchen.

"Yes sir, right away. Oh, I am so terribly sorry," says Nadia as she makes her way to the door, and then quickly hurries down the corridor to find the kitchen. Once in the kitchen she spots Irene and hurries towards her. The kitchen is large with lots of workers preparing food and drinks for guests.

Nadia whispers, "Irine!"

Irine turns and almost drops her drinks at seeing Nadia. Tears well up in her eyes. She's stunned and quickly glances around the room, setting her plate of drinks on the counter.

"Nadia, what are you doing here? It's so wonderful to see you."

She wants to run to her arms, but she knows drawing attention to Nadia would be a terrible mistake.

Nadia whispers, "are there others of us here? I am here with the Prince, and many others. We've come to rescue you and take you home."

Irine looks confused, "The Prince, what Prince? What are you talking about? What others? Nadia, there are armed guards here, it's too dangerous. What Prince?"

"Never mind all that now, how many of us are here and where are they?"

"Darlene, Mary, and - I think – Simone, are all in the last room on the left, down the hall. The others are all upstairs. They only let us older women work tonight. It's some kind of special occasion. They mean to parade out the younger girls and strut them in front of the men."

Nadia says, "Okay, I'm going to make my way back to the others. We are in an empty room down the hall. Can you go upstairs and alert the others we are here and what the plans are. Tell them to open the back window, we can lower them out through there."

Irine nods and scurries up the back stairs.

Nadia grabs a drink from Irine's platter to return to Thomas. She quickly makes her way back and upon entering the parlor, she locates Thomas and presents the drink to him. "Here you are Thomas. Again, I am so terribly sorry. Now if you will excuse me for just a couple more minutes, I must clean myself up as well. But don't you worry, I'll be right back dear."

He grins, "Thank you my dear. I await your return." He looks her up and down, desire in his eyes.

Nadia quickly returns to the dark room. Upon entering, Alexandra is ready with her sword. "It's me," she says.

Gemma steps closer to Nadia, "tell us what you found. Thank heavens you're okay."

Nadia explains, "three of the women are in the next room, and the rest are upstairs to be paraded out like prizes and rented to the highest bidder. Irine went upstairs to notify the girls we're here, and to open the back window in hopes we can lower them down from there."

"Sarah, will you, Alexandra, and Gemma, please go back out the window and figure a way to get the girls upstairs. Nadia and I will get the girls next door."

The girls nod and proceed out the window. Once outside, they look up and see the girls at the second-floor window. They motion to remain silent. Alexandra quickly grabs hold of the ragged wood siding of the old house and scurries up the window to the girls. Her strength and agility are amazing. Once inside she grabs the bed sheets and begins tying them together. The girls all join in, and in minutes they have a strong rope. The girls and Irine make their way down the short distance to the safety of the ground. Gemma smiles and hugs each of them as Sarah points them to the woods.

Meanwhile Nadia and I quietly move down the hall to the next room. Nadia knocks on the door gently, opens it and enters. I follow her. The three women gasp when they see Nadia. I open the back window, greeted by Gemma. Quiet laughter breaks out at the reunion and we all quickly head to the woods.

"Okay, can everyone walk? We have little time and must make it to the Lakehouse." All the captives nod, some wondering who I am.

Gemma remarks, "We'll explain everything, but for now let's get to safety."

Sarah echoes her remark, "Yes, we must hurry before we're spotted."

"Wait, we can't leave the other's," says one of the girls.

"What others? Are there more from Timbervale?" asks Gemma.

"No, not from our village, but prisoners just the same. And the women who work the kitchen, they have all been taken from other villages. Please, we can't leave them."

Gemma looks at me. "We have to help them, James. We've got to try."

"Okay, Sarah, will you escort Nadia, Gemma, and the girls to the Lakehouse? Alexandra, and you there, the girl who spoke up, you come with Alexandra and me. What is your name? You can explain to the other

56

women what is happening and to trust us."

"The girl speaks, "My name is Rachel and yes, I will come with you.

I look to Alexandra, "this is much more complex now and something I had not considered. How will we separate the men in the house from those other women?"

Alexandra thinks for a moment. "If it's true that most of the women are in the kitchen, we need you, Rachel, to go back into the kitchen and inform them to be ready to run to the woods."

"Alexandra, how about you and I starting a little fire in the barn? That should pull the men away long enough for the women to run?"

Alexandra smiles. "Let's do it."

We make our way to the barn while the others head off under the care of Sarah and Gemma. Gemma hugs me, "Be safe James." She then takes off with the group.

Gemma and Sarah all make their way through the back woods and head out for the Lakehouse. People are still out back and out front, laughing and having a wonderful time. Gemma quickly leads them through the narrow streets and then into the forest toward the Lakehouse. So far so good.

The barn has only some hay and grain for horses. We start several small fires, but they spread rapidly. We make our way quickly back to the woods to wait for the others and take cover.

Rachel returns to the kitchen but is stopped by one of the men. "You there, where have you been? What are you doing?"

Rachel replies "I just needed some air; the kitchen is very hot, and I felt weak. But I am better now and returning to my work." She then makes her way towards the back door entrance, leading to the kitchen.

Soon someone screams, "The barn is on fire." Chaos ensues as men scramble to address the fire. Rachel watches and waits, and when clear, she immediately tells the women to go, run, pointing to the woods. She makes a quick pass through the house whispering to other women to run out back as well. She follows behind believing all are accounted for.

Alexandra and I see the woman and we wave them to come this way.

A guard remained at the backdoor and yelled for them to stop, however, luckily in the chaos no one heard him. Alexandra immediately jumped into action attacking the guard. He went down fast as her sword drives deep into his back.

We do a quick check with Rachel and the others, and quickly head off to catch up with Gemma, Sarah and all the others.

I can only hope it is going as well for Orien and Mark.

The Second House

Orien, Mark, Ivan, Luis, and Camilla make their way to the other house hoping to find the women as well. The plan is to get in and out fast and quietly. Arriving at the house, they scope out all sides. There are six people out front, but no guards are seen.

As we make our way to the back of house, Camilla whispers, "There's Italia, Robin, and Salese. Surely others are here as well."

There are also a dozen other people out back so getting in without notice is going to be difficult. This house is much smaller than the one dealt with by the group with James. There is only one floor, but every window is lit up so going in through any of those would be very risky.

Mark speaks up. "Oh, I know a man out front, it's Jackson. He regularly comes to the market so I can join him, and no one will question me. Camilla, how about you come with me since the girls will recognize you? You can act as my evening companion. Orien, Luis, and Ivan hang back, ready to strike if needed."

Camilla nods and she and Mark make their way to the front door. The two lock arms together as if courting each other.

Jackson spots Mark. "Good evening, Mark. We don't usually see you over this way. What brings you out this way, and who is this lovely lady?"

"Good evening, Jackson. This lovely lady is Camilla, a new trader in my market. She lives close to here, and we are just out walking, enjoying the night air. I saw you standing over here so came to say hello."

Jackson takes Camilla's hand kissing the back of it.

Jackson is a dark skinned, older man with greying hair, who has known Mark for many years. He knows Mark has not brought in any new traders, so he's up to something. Jackson turns to the woman with him, "would you be so kind as to get me another drink please, and can you bring one for Mark and Camilla as well?" She leaves, leaving Jackson alone to speak with Mark and Camilla. "Come, let us sit over here."

The three sit at a table a bit away from the others. Mark speaks up. "Jackson my friend. It's good to see you. I am with Luis and Ivan and Prince Edmonds. He's alive and well. We're here to rescue the women brought in from Camilla's village last week. They were kidnapped; taken by force."

Jackson lights up to hear Prince Edmond is alive and well. "The Prince is alive? That is fantastic news. I know the girls you speak of. Most of

59

them are locked in a cage in the basement, though I do not know how many." The girls are well but scared.

"We need to get in the basement. Is there a way in from outside," asks Mark.

"Unfortunately, not. There is an escape tunnel from inside, but it is only accessible from inside the basement. The basement is accessed via a door near the back entrance. If we can draw the ones around back to the front, your friends could slip in."

"That's okay, if there's an escape tunnel from the basement, that's our way out. So, all we have to do is get down there," says Mark. Mark reaches into his bag, pulling out a handful of what look like explosives. He states, "How about a few fireworks to draw their attention out here? Some of the finest from the Orient," he smirks.

Jackson laughs aloud and comments, "why you sly fox. I should have known if you were up to something, it would make a display." Jackson's female companion returns with drinks.

"Everyone, this is my dear friend, Mia."

Mia offers drinks to us all while Mark lights up a cigar, ready to make a scene. He moves to the center of the front lawn and lights off the first firework. An explosion of color lights the night sky. Brilliant orange and white balls accompanied by whirls and bangs capture everyone's attention. Both in the house and in the back of the house.

As Mark continues the show and people begin trickling to the front, Camilla slips to the back. Spotting a few girls from the village, she quickly approaches them, while making hand gestures for them to remain silent.

The two girls are excited to see Camilla. "What are you doing here?" one whispers.

"We're here to take you home. We've been told the rest are downstairs, is this true?"

"Yes, it's true, they keep us locked in a cage down there. Except Genevieve, she's in the kitchen because she can cook."

The men have all made their way out front to see the commotion, so Camilla motions to Orien and the other two to come.

Orien, Ivan, and Luis see Camilla and quickly run to the back entrance. Once there, one girl retrieves Genevieve from the kitchen, and they all quickly make their way downstairs, including a few extra women.

The basement is dark, dingy, and musty smelling. The girls in the cage are thrilled at the sight of Orien and Camilla. "What are you doing here? How did you get here? Can you get us out?" asks one of the girls in the cage, not really expecting any answers.

"MOM!" whispers another girl spotting Camilla.

"Maggie, your safe," says Camilla. "We're going to get you out of there."

Orien asks the girl at the front, "Is there another way out of here without having to return upstairs?"

"Yes, there is a door there, but where it leads, we don't know exactly. We've seen men come and go through it, but only during the day. This cage is locked; we're trapped and only one man we know of has the keys."

Camilla interjects, "there is a tunnel. Jackson told us about it a few minutes ago. That must be the door too it. Can someone try and open it?"

"What were the explosions we heard?" asks one of the girls.

Orien explains it's fireworks as he reaches into his bag. He pulls out a hand full of long sticks that look like dynamite. He chuckles, "These my friends, however, are not fireworks and will make rubble of that cage."

Everyone gets to the back of the cage. Luis and Ivan see if they can get the tunnel door open. "Here's our exit," says Luis.

The men pry the door open and peer in. It is a tunnel, and it's lit by torches. "No sign of anyone. Let's go," says Luis.

The girls all huddle down and plug their ears with their fingers at the back of the cage. "Ready, one, two, three..." Orien lights the fuse. A few seconds later an explosion rocks the house. The men out front all jump and look around. Someone yells. "The women, they've gone after the women." As the men all rush to the basement door, Mark, Jackson, and Mia all make haste in the other direction disappearing into the night.

Ivan had done his best securing the basement door, being the last one to come downstairs. The explosion leaves a lot of smoke and dust, but everyone is okay. Orien and Camilla quickly escort the girls out of the cage and to the tunnel. Ivan and Luis lead the way down the tunnel, preparing for a fight should it become necessary upon exiting the tunnel. The girls race out of the cage and into the tunnel. Orien and Camilla do a quick double check to be sure everyone has gone and bring up the rear.

As they near the end of the tunnel, the torches end, and light can be seen outside. Luis motions for silence as he and Ivan slip out into the darkness. They find themselves in the forest.

"This way! Come this way!" shouts Jackson. He knew where the tunnel opening was and is waiting there with Mark.

The girls all quickly exit the tunnel. Orien, upon entering the tunnel last, lights another explosive and tosses it back. The entrance to the tunnel they had just escaped from quickly collapses. Once all are outside, everyone makes their way to the Lakehouse.

The Reunion

I hear the explosion as our girls, Sarah, Gemma, and Alexandra all make our way to the Lakehouse. We hear yelling and screaming as men still fight the barn fire, and the tunnel explosion. Everyone from both groups' hurries toward home. With all the chaos going on, I hope the men are well delayed in forming a search for us.

At the Lakehouse both groups and all the women meet up. There are hugs, tears, and laughter. Orien speaks up. "All the women, get on the wagons. We must go before they come looking for us. Everyone can finish reuniting enroute to the Cave."

Gemma runs to me and embraces me, "We did it!" she exclaims.

"Yes, but we are not safe yet, we must hurry before they figure out where we have gone. And the sun will be up in only a few hours."

All the women find a place on the wagon and sit. Amelia and Luna did an excellent job filling the wagon with hay, making for a much more comfortable ride. Those of us with horses mount our horses and we all ride into the night toward the cave.

We can only hope that we have enough of a head start that we won't be followed too far in the darkness. That's IF they even figure out which way we were headed. But luck is on our side, and after several hours we arrive home at the cave to the cheers of everyone. The ones asleep at camp quickly jump up as well to greet us all.

Forty-two women in total returned to the camp, thirteen of whom were not from Timbervale, but begged to come. Without question, they were all allowed to come and welcome.

Upon arriving back at the camp, I join the men helping the women off the wagon. Mothers and daughters, and a few husbands and wives, are reunited. Friends laugh and hug, and all rejoice at the success of the evening. Orien comes up and embraces me, "Well done Your Highness."

Then Gemma hugs Orien and everyone else. Laughter and tears are everywhere. Warren welcomes us back, but more importantly reunites with his wife, and of course, Madeline makes a dash scooping up Gemma in her arms welcoming her home. Madeline looks at me and mouths "thank you." I smile and nod.

Sarah comes to my side along with Alexandra. "Very well-done James. You will make a fine King someday." She smiles and hugs me. Alexandra nods, being a little more formal.

I find a tree stump to stand on to be above the crowd.

"Everyone. Everyone, please listen to my words. Tonight, many brave souls and good friends risked their lives to bring these women back to us. And we will forever remember their heroism. Tonight, we took our first stand against Alazaar's wicked rule, and we came out victorious! Tonight, we began to take back our Kingdom and restore my father to his rightful thrown."

The group cheers and claps with still more hugs and tears. "Tonight though...tonight was only the beginning. Our next journey is to bring back our men." Applause and cheers erupt again. "My friends, I came as a stranger to your community. But you accepted me, and more importantly, you trusted me. And I pledge to you here and now I will never ever betray that trust." I raise my sword high in the air. "To Victory." I scream. Once again there is applause and rejoicing among the people.

Gemma comes to my side as I step down from the stump. "Look

around James. Look at the happiness. You did this! You made this happen."

"No Gemma. We made this happen. We all made this happen. And I would not have had the courage without you, Gemma. This community is in your debt."

Gemma blushes at my words and looks away. Glancing back and pausing, then says, "Perhaps Your Highness, but YOU led us. These people followed YOU!"

I smile, looking deep into her brown eyes. "Thank you, Gemma," I softly respond.

"Are you hungry? I am starving and I bet Katherine has food prepared." I put my arm around her, and we begin to walk toward the cave.

"James." I hear my name and turn to see Mark. I lift my arms to embrace him. "Oh Mark, my friend, you must tell me everything that happened at your house. It obviously went well, but when I heard the explosion, I feared for what may have happened."

"James, please meet my friend Jackson, and his lady Mia. And you met Ivan and Luis already. Yes, we must all talk, but first we celebrate."

I hug Ivan and Luis with a man hug, and Ivan remarks, "wow James, I knew you were up to something, but I had no idea to expect this."

"No Mark, first we eat, then we celebrate." I wink.

Mark smiles at my suggestion. "You see my friend; this is why you will make a great King. You think from your stomach." He laughs aloud and pats me on the back. We all head in, in hopes of finding food.

As expected, Katherine is hard at work helping with food and drinks. Several women that were rescued now assisting her. She spots me coming and curtsies. "Your Highness is here," she announces. By now everyone knows who I am, the word spread fast. Inside the cave there are even more greetings and laughter as members of both the rescue groups are welcomed and honored. Katherine and kitchen workers have prepared a feast and has it on the table waiting. Gemma and I reconnect with all the members of both teams at the table, and we all eat, drink, and share all the stories of the evening. The women not originally from the community make their gratitude heard as they are welcomed into full communion as members.

Sarah and Alexandra come up to me after eating. "James, we must be on our way back to my father. I will surely tell him everything that has happened and you can count on all of Westerly to help in your fight."

"Sarah, it is late, are you sure you won't stay until sun rise at least?"

"No, we need to be on our way. I am always safe with Alexandra, and I will sleep better knowing that we are home, and nothing has happened in our absence. Thank you for inviting us to be part of this tonight, we are both honored to have helped."

I hug Sarah and Alexandra, as does Gemma. "We are forever in your debt, and we will certainly continue to stay in touch. If you need anything in the meantime, just send word. Our Kingdom is available for your needs," says Sarah.

An hour later and the sun is rising on a new day. But the events of the night have left everyone exhausted. After everyone has eaten, and all the stories told, almost everyone settles down for some rest and sleep. I walk Gemma to her cot and look her in the eyes again. "You are truly an amazing young woman, and I am in your debt for giving me courage and wisdom to step up and get back at it."

Gemma stares back, and then kisses me goodnight on the cheek.

Laying her hand upon my chest as she says, "Get some rest James." She smiles and my heart skips a beat.

"You too Gemma." I turn and walk to my cot, enamored by her kiss. I lay on my cot, my mind covering the events of the evening. I feel good knowing the women are all safely back. But exhaustion overtakes me quickly. I close my eyes and drift into a deep sleep.

Chapter FOUR: Planning Next Steps

Recovering from Trauma

I don't wake up till late in the afternoon. The camp is quiet with only a few people moving around. I head to the washroom, clean up, and put on clean clothes. Some man comes in and introduces himself. "Your Highness, it's a pleasure to meet you. I'm Ryan. Abbie is my daughter. Thank you for what you have done for our women."

I shake his hand and comment "Thank you, just know that I didn't do it alone; there are many brave people to thank."

"But those brave people went only because you led them Your Highness." He reply's and nods; I can see the gratitude in his eyes.

His words make me feel good, but I know I only went because of Gemma, and the stern admonishment she gave me the night before. Still, I am grateful that we were successful at returning the women. I thank Ryan again for his kind words and make my way to the meeting table.

"Hello Katherine. How are you on this beautiful day? Do you ever rest?"

"Good day Your Highness." She's bubbly, cheerful, and jiggly again. "I get me rest enough. Always something to do though with people in need. Can I get you some coffee Your Highness?"

"Coffee would be great, Katherine. Thank you. Have you by chance seen Gemma today?"

"Indeed, I have. She and her mother were heading to the river earlier.

Not sure if their intent was to fish or bathe, but I'm sure you'll find 'em down there."

I take my cup of coffee and head down to the river. It's another nice day outside and the river is just a short walk. As I approach, I call ahead, "Man alert, are you ladies decent?"

"Yes James, you may come," I hear Gemma yell back. "We are dressed, our bathing complete."

I walk down through the rocks and arrive at the sandy area where the girls are gathered. The river is running rough as it's fed from higher up in the mountains and the ground is rocky. While the river is wide, it is not deep. The water is crystal clear and cold, with the sunshine glimmering like diamonds as the waves rush over the rocks. The forest picks up again on the other side with lush trees and scattered under brush.

Gemma walks over, "Hello James, did you sleep well?"

Madeline echoes, "Good afternoon Your Highness."

"Good day to both of you. Oh wow, I slept so sound I think I may actually have died for a brief period. I was so tired after our return. But I'm feeling really good now. How about you?"

Gemma laughs at my silly comment. "Yes, I was exhausted as well from our trip. And you sir, are the talk of the community today. Everyone is in your debt for bringing back the women."

"As I just told Ryan, I didn't do it, we did it."

"Maybe so James, but we did it because you led us, and you had the plan. You are the hero."

"Okay, okay, you're embarrassing me."

Gemma smiles and laughs.

Madeline states, "She's right Your Highness. You did this."

69

"Well thank you both. Do you know if all the women returned in good health? Were there any injured?"

"All the women are fine James, a few cuts and bruises, but nothing they won't heal from in a couple days. And the ones not from our community are grateful to be here and pledge to work for the freedom they've been granted."

"That's good. We will need all the help we can get to take back our Kingdom. So, Gemma, no more collar. I can promise that. Alazaar will know I had a hand in last night, and he'll be furious the women are gone. If we go back, it will be under the cover of darkness from now on."

"I'm feeling fantastic James. You've given us all hope for a new future. She puts her arm around me and caresses my back. Now we need to rescue the men."

"Yes, indeed we do. But I fear that will be a much more challenging task if they're really at Twin Springs. There's only one way in and one way out. And it's heavily guarded with well-trained soldiers. But first we rest a few days. Let the women deal with the trauma they've been through and spend time with their loved ones."

"That's a wonderful plan," says Gemma, still rubbing my back. "Have you eaten?" she asks.

"No. I have not. I got coffee and came in search of you knowing you would have all the latest information." I laugh.

Madeline speaks up after cleaning some clothes, "Well then come, let us all go eat. We have both our bodies, and our clothes clean now."

"Speaking of clothing, Gemma...the yellow dress you wore the first day I saw you...was it salvageable? You looked so beautiful in it."

Madeline speaks before Gemma has a chance too, "that old dress? I'll have it good as new in no time and she'll be running through the forest trying to catch butterflies while wearing it."

"Mom, I'm not twelve anymore." Gemma rolls her eyes and drops her arms in exasperation at her mother's words.

I laugh aloud, as does her mom. We collect the things and head for food once again. Inside the cave Katherine has fresh biscuits. "I knew you'd be back soon," she says. "Now here you are, fresh biscuits, meat, and some fruit."

"Wow Katherine, your cooking is only outdone by your beauty." I say.

Katherine blushes and points the spatula at me. "Now nobody would get away with flirting with me like that ordinarily, but see-ins you're the Prince, I'll allow it." She laughs and scurries away to get more food for others.

Warren and Orien come over and take a seat. "Your Highness, how are you?"

"Gentlemen, I am well. I trust you all are the same even after yesterday?"

"We are well and excited. There is a new hope in the community. People's fears have been calmed, even if for just a little while. Your plan of two groups advancing under the cover of darkness worked well. And we all returned with no injuries, which is remarkable."

"Thanks, what of Mark and his allies, have you seen them today?" I ask.

"Yes, they returned early and left their compliments, not wanting to wake you. Mark said he had to return quickly, or he would draw suspicion upon himself and others."

"That is true, I'm sure; I will make sure he is properly rewarded for his

71

efforts last night."

Orien replies, "Yes, please do. They were such a big help. We would have had a hard time gaining access to the house without Mark." Continuing, he asks, "So, what about the men? Any new thoughts to share?"

"As I told Gemma earlier, let the women and families have a couple days to rest and process any trauma from the ordeal they've endured. I suspect the younger especially will be having nightmares for several nights. If the men are at Twin Springs, and I believe they are, they are cared for. It's not great conditions, but even Alazaar knows dead men don't mine minerals. A few days won't matter. Plus, the entire city will be on alert after last night. We must give time for things to settle down a little."

"Wise words Your Highness," says Orien. "A few days' rest will be great for everyone. Warren and I got word from our scouts this morning that all is quiet in the forest for now. We can take advantage of that."

"Yes, that is very good news indeed." I turn to Gemma, "so, Gemma, since we have a few days, could you show your Prince around the forest and how you all survive? Maybe introduce me to those I haven't met? Or even put me to work? I'm not too proud to earn my keep around here." I think to myself any of these activities would allow me to spend more time with Gemma and get to know her better. I find myself attracted to her and enjoy spending time with her.

Gemma lights up at my request. "I would love to show you around, James."

We spend the next few days inseparable. We eat together, work in camp together, play together, and enjoy the woods together. She teaches me about all the trees of the forest: oak, pine, walnut, aspen, sycamore, and many others. How to tell them apart. What the wood of each is good for, and which have edible nuts and berries. I am amazed at the knowledge of such things and how folks away from the city survive with skills developed over generations.

Her eyes melt my heart. And when she laughs it's as if the world stops turning. I've had no interest in another woman since my wife's murder, but this beautiful, smart, young woman is captivating.

The Plan

After several days I feel at home here among these people. Their kindness, their dedication to each other, their commitment to rebuilding their lives is genuine. It is here that I have had a few good nights of sleep. Something that has eluded me for many, many months. There is true peace here, the likes of which I believe I have never felt in my life.

I wake up the next morning and head for coffee as usual. Familiar faces smile at me and greet me. Happiness seems everywhere. But I know deep down, everyone wants the men back. And it's time to start developing the plan to get them.

Katherine pours me coffee before I even get to the table. "Another good morning to you Prince James."

I asked that people stop with the 'Your Highness' during every greeting and conversation. I appreciate their respect, but I don't want to be on a pedestal, and the title seems so formal. Gemma came up with 'Prince James' and it seems to have taken hold. I like it. It's simple, respectful, and much less informal.

Orien and Warren come in from making their morning rounds. Both of them work hard to keep supplies coming and going and keep a level of safety around the camp.

"Good morning, Prince James," says Orien.

"Good morning, Orien. Warren. I trust all is well in the camp."

"All is good. We have plenty of food and people have started talking about how to approach rebuilding Timbervale. Their spirits are high, considering the absence of most of the men. Have you thought anymore about a plan to get our men?"

"I have indeed, and I have some ideas. Who here best knows the layout of the Twin springs Mine and its operation?"

Twin Springs is named thus due to the two natural springs that were discovered when the mining operation first started. The hills and mountains of our area provide so many natural resources for our Kingdom; we are truly blessed that our ancestors found this ground centuries ago.

"Actually, I do Prince James. I worked at Twin Springs for several years." Orien says. "What would you like to know?"

Gemma arrives. "Good morning," she says to everyone. "How are you, James?" she asks.

"I'm well Gemma, and you? Orien was just telling me he used to work at the Twin Springs Mine and knows its operation. That's splendid news."

Gemma sits beside me, and Katherine is right there with more coffee, and this time fried ham steaks and biscuits. "Oh, my heavens that looks good. Katherine, you are truly a lady of wonderful surprises."

Katherine giggles. Her bouncy personality is in full display. "Well, it's good to know this old gal still has something to offer."

"My dear Katherine, we would all certainly starve without you." I proclaim.

Warren speaks up, "here's to that for sure. We would all get very hungry without you dear Katherine."

"For sure. We'd have to eat Douglas's cooking. Thank heavens the marauders left you to care for us," says another woman nearby. The room erupts in laughter and we all toast to Katherine, who blushes and returns to her kitchen.

Gemma asks, "So back to the plan, do you have ideas James?"

"I have questions. First, Orien, you said you know the Mine. Do they use rail to transport the raw material?"

"They do Prince James. Rail goes to each level. Cars are filled by hand and pushed by hand to move the material out of the Mine. From there it is transferred to carts and wagons and transported to markets around our Kingdom as well as others."

"And how many levels?"

"There are three levels."

"Perfect, can you draw us a map of each level, please?"

"Absolutely, I'll get right on it."

I turn to Gemma, "you said your community supplied lumber. I guess I know now where the name Timbervale comes from. So, is it fair to say that you had equipment to move large trees, cut them to size, move the slabs of wood, and process it for shipment?"

"Yes, that is correct. Large trees were cut and sawn into dimensional lumber per customer request. Lumber was moved from place to place via a roller and cabling system. James, what are you thinking?"

"I'm thinking about how we can get in, and how we can get the men out. Orien, do we have anyone at Twin Springs who may be sympathetic to our cause?"

"Yes. One of our Women, Tina, is in a relationship with one of the soldiers. His name is Marcus. She travels freely in and out of the Twin Springs Mine."

"How often does she travel there? We should first determine that our men are in fact at the Mine, if Tina can speak with Marcus."

"She has not been since the raid on the village. But we can send her soon to inquire of such."

"Perfect, let's get her there and back safely in the next few days. Next, we need four or five people who are familiar with lumber operations. Warren, can you round up volunteers?"

"Absolutely, I know just who to ask," he replies.

Gemma speaks up, "but James, the entire lumber operation has been destroyed. You saw the ashes. What are you suggesting?"

"Alright, this is what I'm thinking. Everyone please listen. The men in the Mine may be able to dig, but they are not going to be in good health. Some may even be injured. I think we can bring them out using the rail cars. But we can't assume the men will be in good enough health to push the cars, therefore, the cars will need to be pulled out. We can use the cables from the lumber operation and connect them to teams of horses. If the cables are strong enough to move lumber, they will easily pull the cars of men and women on rails. Orien, how many men and women could fit per car? And can the cars be chained together?"

Warren, Orien, and Gemma all look at each other. "That could actually work, but what about all the guards?" asks Warren.

Orien replies, "About fifteen people per car I estimate, and yes, the cars can be coupled together in a chain."

"I have other ideas for the Guards, but first, do we have the volunteers who know the lumber operation?"

"Yes, Your Highness. I am Miranda and these are Allison, Soraya, and Delphine. We worked on the lumber operation daily. How can we help?"

"I would like you all to go back to the remains of Timbervale; the cables used to pull lumber certainly would have survived the fires. Retrieve all the cables you can and bring them back here. Is that feasible? How much time will it take for such an endeavor, roughly? Being safe, we don't want anyone hurt. Maybe leave early tomorrow morning so that you have a full day of sunlight? If you need more than one day, so be it. Take what time is needed."

The ladies all nod. "Oh, and I bet Amelia and Luna with help with that wagon again to transport the cables back here." I add.

Miranda speaks up, "That could be done, but it will take more than one day for sure. There are dozens of cables, all of varying lengths. We do have other women that would be willing to help, with your approval of course."

"Absolutely, I just took a stab when I suggested four of you. You know what the job will require. Those cables will be vital to getting our men."

"We absolutely will help again, Prince James," shouts Luna sitting at a table, overhearing the conversation. "We will get those cables Your Highness."

Miranda says, "We understand, and we will make it happen. All of us know just what to do and how to remove the cables from the old system."

"Would someone please find Tina and ask her to come speak with us?"

Katherine comes over to the table and sets out a couple freshly made pies for folks to enjoy. They smell amazing and Gemma promptly compliments her and thanks her for her effort.

As the pie is sliced and passed around, I get excited. In fact, I get super excited. "That's it!!" I exclaim. "That's our way in. Katherine you're a genius."

Katherine of course looks confused and laughs, wondering what she has done.

Tina arrives, a petite, thin girl with long black hair and dark eyes. She's around my age. She is visibly shy and nervous. "You called for me, Your Highness?"

"Indeed, I did, Tina. Come, sit, let's chat. In fact, have a piece of pie."

Tina smiles, and Gemma helps her get situated and provides her with a slice of pie. "Thank you," she says as she sits across from me.

"Nice to meet you, Tina. It has come to my attention you are in a relationship with one of the Guards at the Twin Springs Mine. I believe they said his name is Marcus, and that because of this you have access to Twin Springs?"

"That is correct Your Highness. Is it wrong of me to be with Marcus? He is a good man, and loyal to our Kingdom, please don't be mad at him. Blame me if our relationship is wrong. Please."

Tina is clearly frightened that I am aware her relationship is with one of Alazaar's guards. Gemma places her hand on Tina's shoulder hoping to comfort her. "Relax Tina," she says.

"Dear Tina. You have the wrong idea of why I've called you. You have done nothing wrong. In fact, it is because you are courting Marcus, I am hoping you will be willing to help us."

"Me? Help? What can I do? I will be glad to help."

"Perfect! First – can you travel to the Mine in the next few days and determine if, in fact, our men really are there? It is vital we know for sure of this before we risk lives in a rescue attempt."

"Oh, I would love to travel to the Mine. I have not been since the raid on Timbervale and wish to let Marcus know that I am okay."

"Good, but I don't want you traveling by yourself, please take people to assist you. I don't want anyone traveling alone anytime soon. Especially our women."

"I can find traveling companions Your Highness; we shall leave tomorrow," Tina replies.

I turn my attention to Katherine. "Hey Katherine, come and sit with us. I have a plan, and it involves you as well."

Katherine stops what she's doing and takes a seat next to Tina. "Me Your Highness, how can I help?"

Turning back to Tina, "Tina, so Marcus is sympathetic to our cause, correct? And we can count on him to help?"

"Oh yes, he is very loyal and hates Alazaar, but to leave the Guard assembly would bring death to him."

"Good, and I don't want him to leave the Guards."

"So, Katherine, in the last few days, Gemma has taught me much about the forest, the trees and the underbrush. She even taught me some of those plants have edible fruit, while others have very poisonous berries." Gemma looks at me with wondering eyes.

"Since you love to bake so much, do you think you and several of the women could bake a batch of pies using poisonous berries? Then Tina, if you could alert Marcus, I think the Guards deserve a nice dinner and dessert, compliments of Alazaar. Maybe some sandwiches and pies? What do you think?"

Everyone is shocked as the idea takes root. Gemma and Katherine both sit there with their mouths open. Orien and Warren start to laugh. And Tina just stares at me.

"How about it Tina? Do you think you can get Marcus to work with us to poison the Guards?"

She smiles and chuckles. "Absolutely Your Highness, I guarantee he would love to poison several of them."

Gemma smiles, "Wow James, that's a fantastic idea."

"Poisonous Pies? Now that's something no one has ever requested of me before," says Katherine. "But you bet we can do it. We'll make those soldiers the best looking, best smelling pies they've ever laid eyes on. And with enough sugar, and a mix of edible berries, they'll have no idea their dessert is deadly." She begins to laugh and says while looking around the room, "Girls, we're going to need lots of pie crust dough and lots of berries from the woods."

"Awesome. Don't start yet though, we have to coordinate all the timing of everything. Orien, we're going to need a way to attach those cables to the cars, can I leave that to you, please? I'm hoping the cables that were used at the lumber system can be connected to the rail cars in some manner. Oh, we going to need some more of those explosives like you used to blow up that cage as well."

"I can take care of all that, drawings, explosives, and cable ties for the cars. You shall have it."

Madeline speaks up. "I'm with you Katherine, we girls will help with all those pies."

Tina says, "Thank you sir, for being so understanding."

I nod, wink, and smile at her.

"Orien, one last question. You said the Mine has three levels. Are there air ventilation shafts to each level?"

"There are, but if you're thinking of using them for entry or exit, they are way too small for that."

"Nope, not for people. I have another idea."

"Very well then, the engineering is being worked to extract everyone; a team is going after cables; and we have a plan to eliminate the guards and get access to the Mine. We will need wagons to transport the men back here again as well."

Luna shouts again, "You can count on us for that too Prince James, but we'll need two wagons for all the men."

"Two sounds terrific. Thank you Luna, you knew I was going to ask." She waves and I chuckle.

"All that's left is where to house everyone after the men return. This cave is barely big enough to hold the women that returned. We need more space."

Warren speaks up again, "Oh no Prince James, this cave is huge. You've only seen the small part that we have lit. Come let us show you; be prepared to be amazed."

"He's right James. We are only using a small portion of this cave because it's all we needed. Come, let us show you the rest of it," says Gemma.

"I'd love to see it. Is there anything else we need to discuss?"

"Just the timing Prince James," says one of the women. "I am Madison, and I was in that cage last night and rescued by Orien and Mark.

I want revenge and I want my husband back."

"And you shall have both."

"Today is Thursday. I know it will take several days to prepare everything and finalize all the details. I think the Guards would be open to an end-of-week celebration from their beloved Alazaar for their hard work. What does everyone think of a week from tomorrow? Next Friday? Sound feasible?"

"I can certainly have the food prepared by then," says Katherine.

"And we'll have those cables back by the end of the weekend and be working on how to splice them and prep for connection to the cars," says Miranda.

Orien says, "Sounds like great planning. Well done everyone."

"Come James, let's show you the rest of the Cave," says Gemma.

Everyone claps and cheers. Then the group breaks up, each picking a task they can do to help the effort. Gemma comes and puts her arm around me. "You are a natural leader James, and an absolute genius. This is going to work my Prince."

"Her Prince?" I like the sound of that, I think to myself.

With the plans established we get up from the table and turn toward Orien. "Lead the way."

I take Gemma's hand, and we follow Orien to the back left of the cave. A couple of the men move several rocks exposing a passageway while others hand out torches. Orien leads the way. We walk a short distance as Warren explains how the passageway could easily be widened for easier access. Soon we exit the passageway and enter into an enormous cavern. It's beautiful and lit by natural sunlight from the chasms above. At the bottom is water. I see a small lake that is being fed from waterfalls on the cavern walls, then running back out to the river below.

I am in awe. "Wow! This is absolutely stunning. We could fit the entire village in here."

"Yes, that is why this site was chosen as our emergency shelter, but with so few survivors last week, coming in this far wasn't necessary, so we just blocked the passageway and used the front part," says Warren.

I can't get over the size and beauty before me. I squeeze Gemma's hand. She says, "I didn't mean to keep this place a secret James, it just didn't occur to me to show you because we've not needed it. Plus, I couldn't have moved the stones to get back here anyway, but we have plenty of room for everyone. It'll just take some work to get settled, but we will also have the men back to help. They are all familiar with the cavern."

"No worries at all, I completely understand. This will take care of all of us for sure. And the security it will provide. That ceiling has to be a hundred feet up."

We all walk back to the main table and sit down. My mind is going over so many details. But I know it will all come together; I have faith in this community.

As I sit down, I look for Orien. "One more thing, Orien. The explosives, I don't want to blow anything up, I just want to send up flares. Can the explosives be reworked to make a show without a lot of destruction?"

"I'm sure we can produce something like that. We'll have it all ready."

Katherine brings a round of beer as I remark. "Well, everyone, I believe we have our plan."

Chapter FIVE: Mining for Men

Preparation for Danger

Gemma hugs me. "That's some amazing planning. You've really thought it all through, and the way you've involved so many people. Everyone is so excited to support you and get our men back. But what about you? How are coping with all of this? I hope you know I fully support you."

"Thanks Gemma. I know that, and it means a lot. You know you have changed my whole life and given me a new life I wasn't expecting. I still think many young women, would have taken off and not forgiven me for 'buying' them. Oh, how I wish I could have met you under different circumstances."

"James, we often don't get to choose what fate hands us. But you have been honorable and courageous. You have taken a community left in ashes and given us hope. You have shown us all that there is so much more to our lives than just what happens in Timbervale, and I, personally, am developing feelings for you. I can't keep it a secret. You are making me feel things I've never felt for any other man James."

I blush feeling a rush of emotions overtake me, but I keep my composure. "Thank you, Gemma. You are indeed a beautiful, intelligent, young woman, with a huge heart and a true spirit of courage as well. I am developing feelings for you also. From the moment I saw you in that stupid cage, my heart became attached to you. And I couldn't do any of this, none of it, without you."

She comes and wraps her arms around me, and we just hold each other. I never want to let go, but we have much work to do. "You won't have to do it without me James. I'm not going anywhere."

I brush her hair out of her eyes and caress her face with my fingers. Her skin is soft, her eyes chocolate brown that sparkle in the fire lit cave. She is a few inches shorter than me, and thin, but not skinny. "Come, let's help Warren with the passageway." I take her hand, and we walk to the entrance of the cavern.

Warren and several others are clearing rock and working to widen the passageway connecting the cave to the cavern. While the cave may be eight to ten hectares, the cavern is every bit twenty-five hectares. There is so much room we could grow crops in here.

"Prince James, Gemma, have you come to help?" asks Warren.

"We have indeed. I'm not much of an engineer, but I have two strong arms. How can I help?"

"I can help too, and I am not afraid of work. Tell me how I can assist." Gemma adds.

Warren introduces the women and a couple of men once more to Gemma and me. Then he explains the concept of the new passageway, as well as the required bracing to keep it all safe. Without further a due we all keep busy.

The passageway is only about two meters in height, and a meter wide. The sides are a combination of loose rock and limestone boulders. The idea is to break it all apart so that it becomes three meters high and four meters wide. That will take a lot of bracing, which they want to cut from trees. Having run a lumber mill, no question they have the skills to accomplish the task.

I help with moving the rock while Gemma puts her skills to use helping other women with the lumber. She knows wood and how to cut it and prepare it using hands tools they brought from the village. She is a skilled craftsman for sure and assists with not only the doing, but the planning and architecture as well.

Meanwhile, Orien and a group have been developing a method to attach the cables to the cars. They rig up a furnace outside the cave to heat and shape metal fittings that can be used to secure everything together. The furnace is comprised of several rocks extracted from the passageway. They all know how to use everything around them and I am truly impressed.

Miranda and her team also stay busy mapping out where the cables are, how they will disconnect them, and how to categorize them by thickness so as to properly withstand the stress of pulling the cars.

Katherine starts figuring out how much flour she will need to make a dozen pies. There are usually twenty-five to thirty guards in the Mine at any given time. So, a dozen pies should be plenty, and thirty-five sandwiches made with sliced ham just for extra.

After many hours of work, Katherine's kitchen help rings the dinner bell. We are all tired and hungry. There is still much to do, but everyone got a good start.

I meet back up with Gemma and we go to eat. As usual on heavy workdays, a feast has been prepared and set out for everyone. Katherine has eight others that have helped, having been rescued the night before. And although all are tired, there are nothing but smiles and laughter to be seen and heard.

I ask Gemma how it went with building the wood supports.

"It was super fun. I've missed making sawdust and being productive. We all had a good time and completed two supports. How did the rock moving go?"

"I doubt I had as much fun as you did, but it was good. Hard work for sure and my arms hurt, but I can't complain. A little embarrassed several of the women moved a lot more rock than I did."

Gemma laughs, "Our poor Prince, outdone by the women."

"It's true, I admit defeat." I hang my head in mock shame as Gemma giggles at my embarrassment.

Everyone takes a seat to eat. Orien sits across from us. "I went over by the passageway, you all made good progress," he says.

Gemma pipes in, "thanks to the women." She looks at me and laughs again. I chuckle at her and wink.

"How did the furnace building go?" I ask.

"It went well. We'll be melting metal tomorrow," says Richard, the blacksmith of the community.

Others speak up about how the day went while we eat, and what was accomplished. Everyone is proud of the team they were on, and the friendship that was shared today.

After dinner Gemma and I go for a walk. She's extra happy tonight, once again having a productive day. She dances around reciting a song she's familiar with. I enjoy watching her, and long for the day everyone can be so happy.

Gemma senses I am concerned about things, so she invites me to sit beside her on a dead tree, fallen in the forest. I join her. The sun has set, and the air is cool. Fireflies fill the air with their florescent lights twinkling like fairies across the night sky. Gemma takes my hand, and we just sit there and enjoy the quiet. She breaks the silence, "Hello. James? You seem far away, are you okay?"

"I'm fine." I squeeze her hand and smile. "Just tired from a full day's work."

"James, I can tell you're concerned. What is it?"

"You see right through me don't you." I say rhetorically. "Yes, I am worried about the men and what happens after. People will die in this rescue; that I fear is certain, and I don't know if we can stop it."

Gemma kisses my fingers. "No one expects you to stop it. This is going to be dangerous, and everyone understands the risk. Your concern for everyone is honorable, but you can only do what you can do. You've started us on a path that everyone is excited to walk with you. When I first saw you, from inside that stupid cage, I could see the concern in your eyes. I could tell that for some reason, I was going to be okay. It is true, I was scared, and tired, and wet, and cold, so I tried to act tough, but you were not like the others that stared at me in that cage. That's why I never ran. You care about people, and it shows. You have to know that you are not doing this alone."

I lay my head on her shoulder. "Thank you, Gemma. Your support means more than you can possibly imagine. I do care. These people are so kind. They are all good people, and they didn't deserve what happened."

She puts her hand on my head, and I close my eyes. For a moment I relax, not wanting this moment to end. Gemma has more courage than anyone I've ever met, and I'm touched that she's come into my life.

We spend some more time chit-chatting about the activities of the day and what's coming up in the next week. After a while I stand up and take her hand. "Okay my dear, let's head back and see if anyone's at the community table."

We head back and hear the laughter and noise of a group of people. Katherine and some women are serving beer, and everyone is relaxed and joyous. Gemma grabs my hand and pulls me to the area where others are dancing. We dance together in the company of all the others and share a cold beer. The dangers of the future do exist, but for tonight, we are happy, safe, and filled from a fantastic meal. I put my worries away and enjoy the moment and the beautiful woman in front of me.

The next day starts early with the same routine. Coffee at the community table and discussion about what the day will bring. Gemma and Madeline are both already up and helping, and before long Orien and Warren arrive from their morning rounds. Gemma smiles as I approach and greets me, "Good morning, Prince James."

"Good morning, everyone."

Miranda and several women approach. "Good morning, Prince James. The horses and wagons are ready, as are we, to go begin the extraction of the cables. We have weapons with us should we need them, but we pray for a peaceful and productive trip."

"Very well Miranda, thank you, thank all of you for stepping forward to do this. Please stay safe and come back before sunset."

"Yes, Your Highness, we shall see you tonight before sunset." They turn to leave and Gemma steps forward giving them hugs and well wishes. A short while later they are on their way.

A few men fire up the furnace to pour metal today and the group that worked on the passageway return to work after having some breakfast.

Gemma then gives me a hug before returning to the mill area to work on more support beams. I sit with Orien and go over the drawings of Twin Springs, and his thoughts about how to connect the cars and cables using the metal parts being forged in the furnace today. Everything continues as planned.

A short while later Tina and two women come, ready to leave. "We are set to head to the Mine. I shall inform Marcus of everything we've discussed. I know he will be excited for this to happen. I look forward to introducing you to Marcus someday."

"Safe travels. See if you can get an idea of how many Guards or Soldiers work the Mine now-a-days. Especially at night."

"I will and report back. And don't worry about my safety, if anything happened to me, people know Marcus would cut their heads off, slowly and painfully," she giggles.

I nod, not really knowing what to say after that.

Orien, Ryan, Margaret, and a few others tend to make the molds for the furnaces, ready to cast old pieces of steel from the village that can be scrapped. After the attack, several of the folks had returned to Timbervale to salvage what they could, not really knowing what could be useful at the cave. Thus, there is some old equipment and tools that can be melted to make clasps. After all that, I return to the passageway as well and begin the chore of more rock removal.

The time passes quickly, and I am not used to such work unfortunately, so by midafternoon I go check on Gemma. She is hard at work, milling down a huge piece of lumber. Her hair hangs down over the sides of her face as she planes away the wood. The work clothes she's wearing covered in sawdust and grime, she is unaware I'm watching her. My fondness for her continues to grow, but I know we must stay focused on getting the men back. Now is not the time for romance. Still, I wonder what the future could hold for us if anything at all.

I walk closer, and she looks up. Her smile is infectious. "Hello James, what are you up too?"

"I had to take a break. Those rocks are beyond heavy. And I was just thinking about you and how you're doing. Your task looks daunting."

She laughs, "This is fun work. I enjoy creating things. It was sweet of you though to come check on me. Thanks." She looks down at her clothes, "I suppose I'm not much to look at right now." She looks at me and grins.

"I think you are the most beautiful girl I have ever seen. No matter what you are wearing." I brush sawdust out of her hair.

"Oh yes, covered in sawdust, tree bark, and dirt. I'm sure it's the look you dream of at night." She busts out laughing and waves me off.

"So, want to show me what you're doing?" I ask.

"Would you like to try? Have you ever used a hand plane?"

"I haven't used any type of tool. But I'd love to learn. My studies were music and swordsmanship."

"Really? You're a musician? And a swordsman? You told me you had no combat training."

"Using a sword against tutors who dare to injure you, verses against a trained soldier who want to kill you, are two very different things."

"I suppose you're right" she says. She hands me the plane, "here let me show you." I take the plane and look it over. "Now, what you want to do is remove shavings of the wood until we have it at the desired thickness. Come on, put it on here."

I place the tool on the wood and prepare to push. "Not like that. You will cut too deep into the wood." She places her hands over mine and rotates the tool just slightly. "The idea is to let the tool do the work. So, we want to push forward gently. Not down, thus letting the blade cut the slice."

She guides my hand moving the tool several times. At first the tool tends to grab the wood, but with a little practice we are slicing very long thin pieces of wood from the lumber. "There, now you have the idea. You work now and I'll watch" she says playfully, laughing again.

"I am supposed to be on break," I say jokingly. She just grins and rolls her eyes in her head.

Meanwhile, back at Timbervale, the group is making good progress collecting the cables. There are several dozen cables running all throughout what was the lumber mill. And while everything is covered in ash, and memories abound, the group goes about their business determined to get as much done as they can in one day. It's hard work, but the cables disconnect relatively easy. They are just long and heavy. The team started with the longest ones, knowing they would be of the most use according to the plan.

As the afternoon closes, the team loads up what cables they can and heads back to the cave in order to arrive before the sun sets. Almost all the cables have been disconnected. One return trip tomorrow will allow them to gather the rest fairly quickly. Luna's wagon makes easy work of transporting the cables back to the cave.

While Gemma continues to coach me on carpenter skills, several of the passageway workers notice, and tease me. "Work him hard Gemma. Don't let him off easy just cause he's too weak to move rocks all day."

Gemma shouts back, "don't you worry. I've not let him slack up from the work." Everyone laughs and has an enjoyable time.

An hour later Miranda's team arrives with the cables. Everyone stops to help unload the wagon and tend to the horses. "How did it go I ask?"

"It went very well Prince James. A short trip tomorrow and we shall have them all." Orien looks at the cables, "I was concerned what kind of shape these would be in after the raid. Between horses' hooves, the chaos of the fighting, and then the fires, I feared the worst. But these are really in decent shape and will certainly pull those cars. We should have plenty of length too. Very nice," he says.

"Well done ladies. Be sure to get some rest and eat well tonight, you've earned it today for sure." The ladies all nod and head to see what Katherine has prepared.

No sooner than Gemma and I get cleaned up than I hear someone calling. "Prince James, Prince James, may we speak with you?"

I turn and see Tina. She walks up, "Prince James, I'd like you to meet Marcus. He really wanted to meet you, so he managed to return with me."

Marcus goes down on one knee and bows his head. "Your Highness, it is an honor. I knew your father well. When Tina told me of everything that has happened, I had to come to pledge my allegiance Your Highness."

"Welcome Marcus. It is indeed nice to meet you and nice of you too come. Thank you, Tina, for your bravery. Come, you must both be hungry, let us go and eat. But before we do, Marcus, please let me introduce Gemma."

"Gemma, Tina has spoken much about you and what you have done for this community. Both before and after the raid. Lucky for you, Your Highness saw you in that cage."

"It was fate, and yes, I am blessed. Now come, let's eat." Gemma remarks

We arrive to the gathering area as Katherine is directing the final setups for dinner. Marcus is introduced to Orien, Warren, and several others. His is a big man, with muscular arms. His hair is golden blonde, short, and curly. He is wearing the standard Guard uniform. He and Tina have a seat with us at the main table. Tina's friends come up and welcome her back.

"So, Marcus, Tina has told you of our plan to rescue our men?"

"Yes, Your Highness. And I have shared these plans with only a few others I trust with my life. We are excited and willing to help."

"It is good you trust them with your life. If they betray us, it could cost us all our lives, but I trust Tina has made a wise choice in choosing you as her escort."

Tina smiles and hugs Marcus.

"Yes, Your Highness, Alazaar will have our heads if he finds out about this," Marcus replies.

Orien speaks, "Marcus, I worked the Mine for years. You know of our desire to pull the men, women, and loyal guards from the Mine using the rail cars. And you think this will work?"

"I do Orien. While the Mine has grown larger and deeper since you were there, the basics are the same. The rail goes through each level. There a six cars per level, plenty enough to extract everyone."

"Are any of the men injured?" asks Gemma.

"Yes, I am sorry to say. The men have not been treated well and mining is demanding work. There have been a few accidents, but most are well."

"Have any been killed?" She follows up with a shakiness in her voice.

"No Gemma, all the men are still alive."

Some of the women in the room begin to cry hearing that their husbands and sons are still alive. Gemma bows her head, nodding in gratitude.

We all talk as we eat and go over all the plans in great detail. In addition, we try to think through alternative plans based on anything and everything going wrong.

Marcus speaks up again. "Your Highness, I want to be honest. Your plans are solid, but there will still be risk. Most of the Guards are very loyal to Alazaar. If things go wrong, men could die."

"I understand the risks."

Miranda speaks, "We all understand the risks. But we want our husbands and sons back." The room breaks out in cheer.

I return to speaking, "I do understand the risks, we all do, but we must fight to take back our Kingdom and restore my father to the throne." Again, the room erupts in applause.

With that Gemma wraps her arms around my arm and Tina smiles at Marcus who replies, "Very well then, let us toast to victory."

"To Victory!!"

Gemma leans her head on my shoulder. I can sense the fear of the unknown, but also confidence in our people and our plan.

Marcus says, "Your Highness, I must return to the Mine. Tina will return to the Mine in three days' time, and I will make her aware of any changes."

"That sounds wonderful. Thank you both once more for your bravery."

Katherine says, "Okay, everyone be on your way for the evening so we can clean up. Breakfast will be here before you know it."

"You heard the lady, let's take it all outside tonight."

Everyone makes their way out of the way. Many assist with the cleanup. I look at Gemma. She takes my hand and leads me outdoors. There we all talk in more detail of the day's planned events. Warren says he expects enough rock will be removed tomorrow to start securing bracing. The furnaces were a success, and the coal fire easily got hot enough to melt the metal scraps. There are a lot of smiles and laughter, as everyone takes pride in what is being accomplished.

Gemma and I sit on a tree stump and just enjoy some time together.

Over the next few days, flour is ground, berries are picked, the other cables are gathered, more fittings are forged, the passageway is completed, and Tina returns to Marcus to learn of any complications.

Gemma comes up to me and rests her intertwined arms on my shoulder. "Well James, isn't it amazing?"

"It is indeed. My father would be so impressed with all of this. I wish he could see it."

"He will soon enough. And he will be immensely proud of you James and how you've motivated everyone to make this work," she says.

I blush. "Thank you, Gemma."

Tina returns the next day and reports all is well. We begin plans for the cavern, hoping to make it the new village and lumber mill. Timbervale arose generations ago in that spot in the forest, and it served the community well. But rebuilding in the same spot makes no sense with the natural security and pleasantness of the cavern.

There will still be outdoor buildings necessary, and a second entrance will be required for lumber operations. Coming through the cave, even with a wider passageway, is certainly not practical.

A week has passed, and it is Thursday morning. Our rescue operation is set for tomorrow night, and everyone and everything will be finalized today. I stare at the ceiling of the cave over my cot, as I lie there waking up. "Coffee. I need coffee," I think to myself.

I stumble back to the kitchen and make small talk with Katherine. Gemma comes in, stretching and smiling. She is always so happy. I extend my arm to offer her a hug, which she happily accepts. "Good morning James."

"Good morning. What are we forgetting? I couldn't sleep last night, for worry that we're missing something."

"James, you've got this. Everyone has worked so hard this past week. But I do understand it is your place to be concerned."

I lean my forehead against her forehead. "You're awesome." She just smiles at me.

The rest of the day we touch base with every person in the community. I extend admiration to each and every one of them personally. There is both excitement and fear. Of the people now present at the cave, thirty are headed to the Mine tomorrow. That's ten people per level in the Mine to distribute the pie and sandwiches and to assist the captured men. And, if any fighting is necessary to eliminate the threat of the whatever Guards are around, we stand a chance of defeating them.

Those remaining here will set up first aid centers to assist everyone who returns as needed. We have food, water, bandages, splints, everything we can think of that may be needed.

Amelia and Luna have two wagons, hoping to bring back the thirty-one men that were taken from the village.

The cavern is far from being settled, but there is safe ground and plenty of room for everyone. It will take months to resettle everyone, but for now, the cavern will provide shelter and security as is.

Gemma shares a smile with each person as well. She is so strong and capable of bringing people together and having a good time while she does it.

Orien has been very successful configuring the cables to attach to the cars, and creating three bundles of cabling, one for each level.

The pies smell amazing, even if they are deadly. Katherine has done an amazing job as well.

The day goes by fast as we tend to all the last-minute details. By nighttime, Gemma and I are both once again, very tired and resting on our favorite tree stump. She takes my hand intertwining her fingers with mine. "Are you okay?" she asks.

"I am, actually. I can't think of anything we're not prepared for. I can't tell you often enough what your support through all of this has meant to me. But, if I die tomorrow, there's still one thing I will have regretted not doing."

"What's that James?"

I put my arm around her and pull her close. She turns and looks at me, and I am captured by her beautiful eyes. As I look intently at her, feeling her body's warmth next to mine. I lean toward her, and our lips meet for the first time. She embraces the kiss, and it becomes passionate as her arms pull me close. Our eyes closed, our tongues dance in ecstasy as our mouths melt together. My heart is racing, as time stops, and all our worries disappear if but only for a brief period.

As we break this kiss, for need of air, we stare at each other and smile.

"That!"

"I would have regretted not having done that, Gemma."

She smiles and blushes heavily, clearly a little embarrassed at my action. "Was that okay? Forgive me if I was too forward."

"Oh, it's not that at all James. It was wonderful. I've just... I've just not ever kissed a man like that before. I'm glad it was with you James."

"But you better not die tomorrow," she adds.

We both chuckle.

The Rescue

The next morning brings both anxiety and hope. There is an unspoken excitement as everyone prepares for the final stretch, The plan is to arrive at the Mine just after sunset, hoping for less security to deal with by that hour. Marcus will be there to greet us and help us feed only the corrupt guards the poison pies. We have good pie for those still loyal to the King.

The standard morning crew meets for coffee. Only today is more small talk than planning. We trust everyone has done their part, now we need to stay out of their way and let them work. I meet Gemma in the kitchen, "Good morning sunshine."

"Sunshine? Do I brighten your day James," she jokes.

"Gemma my dear, you brighten everyone's day."

She chuckles and gives me a hug. Then we get coffee and walk around as everyone is finishing packing for our trip. "James, what do you think tomorrow will be like?"

"Tomorrow? I've been so focused on this day for so long, I've not stopped to consider tomorrow."

"I know. Which is why I'm asking. It will come - be it good or bad."

"I choose to think tomorrow will be a day of celebration as the loved ones are all reunited. Tomorrow will be a new beginning, for all of us, but tomorrow will also be the first day we are officially at war with Alazaar."

"I never thought of it that way," she replies.

"We have a long journey ahead of us."

Orien walks over. "Prince James, good morning. We have the cables all loaded. They are already attached to the wagons, so it's simply a matter pulling them throughout the Mine and attaching the cars."

He continues, "The pies and sandwiches are stored in the covered wagon and ready to go. Tina and a few women will get a head start and connect with Marcus. If anything has changed, she will ride back to us and let us know quickly. And the explosives have been readied and staged with the groups of cables, just like you asked."

"Well done, Orien. We would never have pulled this off without you, my friend."

"It's been a privilege Your Highness," he responds.

Between mid-morning and early afternoon everyone gets some rest, knowing it will be a long night. The plan is to leave by late afternoon, prepared for the three-hour journey by horse and wagon. The Mine is northeast of Artems, so closer, but still a long journey.

Gemma and I go and sit by the river, throwing stones into the water, just relaxing together. We eat a sandwich as well and close our eyes for a brief period. She lays her head on my shoulder as we lay there in the sandy area. I am totally at peace feeling the warmth of her body against mine, while having my arm around her.

After some needed rest, we all gather together, do a final check, and head to the Mine. The laughter and smiles have been replaced by focus and concern. We face a daunting task, but to have the community fully reunited will make it all worth it. I assist Gemma mounting her horse, and then mount mine.

Moving to the front of the caravan I wave my hand to get attention. "My dear friends, we now embark on the second journey to reunite our families and community. We face risk, and danger, but I believe we will be victorious. You all have worked hard preparing for this moment, and you are ready." I raise my sword in the air. "Tonight, we return with your men," I scream.

Everyone cheers in support. I look at Gemma, she smiles and says, "well said James." I pull on the reins and we begin our journey.

As we travel through the forest, I can't help but think of the beauty and peace of the moment. My mind weighs what will be in the coming months and what wrath Alazaar will bring upon us. But I know we will face it together and I can depend on Gemma to be by my side. I think about the kiss last night and how my heart felt as her lips met mine.

Gemma asks, "You're smiling. What are you thinking about?" She had just been watching me apparently as we move forward.

I blush. "I was thinking about our kiss last night and how important you are to me. And the fate which has led me here and to you."

Again, she blushes. "I'm glad I'm here, James."

I reach from my horse to hers and take her hand. "I'm glad I'm here too."

We arrive at the outskirts of the Mine, remaining well out of sight in the forest. The sun is setting indicating we are right on time. Before long, Tina arrives from the Mine and greets us. "How was your journey she asks?"

Gemma responds, "It was good, is Marcus ready for what we have planned?"

"Yes, word has spread to the loyalists, and everyone is ready. I will escort the wagon."

I wave for Katherine and the women serving food to approach. Katherine maneuvers the wagon and crew to the front. Tina greets her, "Hello Katherine, are you ready?"

"We are very ready. Let's do this." She starts to move everyone with her forward. Tina dismounts and climbs aboard the covered wagon with Katherine, tying her horse to the back of the wagon.

"Good luck and God speed, we'll be right behind you."

It's only a short distance to the entrance to the Mine. Tina rides up front in the wagon with Katherine as she drives, followed by the women to assist her. A distance behind, the rest of us remain out of sight, as we don't want to raise unnecessary concern among the guards.

As the wagon approaches, Marcus and two Guards come from the entrance and stop them. Marcus plays his part and interrogates Katherine. He orders the other two soldiers to search the wagon. "Just pies and sandwiches as they claimed," he reports.

"Very well, continue. The men will appreciate your gesture." They all move forward to the entrance of the Mine, and all dismount. The other women are searched for weapons. Gemma, the others, and I stay far enough away that we can see without being noticed.

After Katherine and Tina move into the cave, Marcus explains to the

Guards that the women have brought sandwiches and pies to say thanks to all the Guards for the arduous work they provide to the Kingdom. The women fan out to all the levels and start serving the food to the men. Each of the guards are grateful for the meal and assist in getting the food to all the guards on all the levels. The poison in the berries is extremely potent and takes effect 10 - 15 minutes after consumption. The Nightshade berries resemble blueberries only darker and more bitter, a characteristic easily covered by sugar and a sauce made from edible berries.

As the food is passed around, the guards make rude gestures and catcalls to the women, eliminating any guilt the women have of bringing them to their demise.

Unfortunately, the time it takes to distribute the food means the men closest to the entrance have eaten by the time it arrives to the last men on the third level. The men working recognize the women but ignore them to keep everyone safe.

A rider, a scout, approaches quickly toward Gemma and I. "Alazaar's men approach. Still a thirty-minute ride, but fifty soldiers are on their way." Orien overhears, "Prince James, we have to move now or face certain death."

I unsheathe my sword, "We ride now." I kick the horse, and we all take off to the entrance at top speed. As we arrive, Marcus and the loyal Guards, unsure of why we are approaching so fast, know that something has changed. I arrive at the entrance met by a Guard with his sword drawn. Marcus comes from behind and thrusts his sword into the guard. The man falls to his knees and then on his face. Another guard blows a whistle and the fight is on. The poison is obviously having an effect as the soldiers try to engage.

"Alazaar's soldiers are on the way. Fifty estimated, we must move now." I explain to Marcus.

"The food has probably not been fully consumed on all levels yet so we can expect a fight," says Marcus. Orien and his men, along with the wagon pull up. "I heard" he says. "Let's go guys." The men jump into action and begin pulling cables into the Mine.

A guard makes his way down the tunnels alerting the others, "Attack, attack. We're under attack."

A few men from the community healthy enough to fight spring into action, and the fight ensues. Luckily, many of the guards did eat the pie, and are sluggish as they wield their swords, making easy work for the men to defeat them.

Gemma jumps from her horse and runs into the Mine along with all the other women. Each team makes their way to their assigned levels to assist the men. The men on the lower levels have a harder fight as not all the guards had a chance to eat, however, the loyal guards assist and quickly defeat those loyal to Alazaar.

Cables get connected quickly to rail cars and men that are too weak to walk are lifted into the cars along with the women that came to help. Gemma makes her way to the second level and spots her father. She runs to embrace him as tears flow down her face. Her father firmly holds her in his arms, "Gemma, my dear Gemma, you're alive. But what are you doing here? It's so dangerous."

"Yes father, I'm alive and so is Mom, and it's a long story we shall share later."

Someone yells, get in a car. Gemma's dad lifts up Gemma and sets her up in a car. Then helps the other men and women on that level.

Per the plan, the focus was on the third level, being the hardest to extract. Warren and his team make a clean sweep of the level. Once everyone is safely in cars, Warren approaches the ventilation shaft and lights the explosives provided by Orien. A perfect explosion shoots flames up the air shaft, and like a fireplace, the flames are quickly drawn upward and out. The flames are easily visible to those outside and provide the signal that the third level is ready. Shortly after, the explosives are ignited by the second level team, shooting flames out the second level air shaft. The women driving the wagons leap into action and take off.

As the wagons leap forward, the cables all pull tight, and the rail cars lunge forward on the rails. The occupants all hold tight as their ride begins. Gemma hugs her dad tightly and closes her eyes. A few minutes later and all the cars are outside the Mine. Those in the top level either walk out or are placed in the covered wagon.

Everyone moves quickly as men and women move from rail cars to wagons. All get settled as they prepare to take off for the cave. Gemma hugs her dad and explains she has her horse, and that she will catch up with him back at the Cave.

"The cave, why at the cave?" he asks.

"I'll explain later dad," she yells back while running to her horse.

Her dad takes a seat on a wagon and gets comfortable, and the caravan heads home.

I have the reins on Gemma's horse and wait for her. Marcus and Tina come out of the cave riding together on Tina's horse.

"We've made a pass through the cave; everyone is out," Marcus says.

"Very well, let's go."

The four of us take off, leaving the Mine and dead soldiers behind. We all ride fast putting a great deal of distance between us and the Mine before Alazaar's soldiers arrive.

We all ride hard for about an hour, but there's no indication we're being followed, or if Alazaar's soldiers even arrived at the Mine. Everyone is tired but excited. Lots of hugs take place on the wagons, with more laughter and smiles again, but there are men that were injured and in need of care.

Another hour later and we see Orien on the side waiting for us as the bulk of everyone passes by. "Orien, how is everyone? I felt it best for us to remain in the rear in case anyone has to stop."

"I am well, and my spirits are up. The people are tired, especially the men from the Mine. They are malnourished and weak, but they will recover."

"That's excellent news, Orien."

"We did lose three people Your Highness. Two men and one woman in the fighting."

Gemma gasps while I hang my head in sorrow. "Thanks for letting us know Orien."

Gemma speaks up. "That's terrible, I must find out who and speak to their families."

"We shall both speak to their families."

The news of three deaths is sobering, but considering everything, it could have been much worse. We continue on, arriving back at the cave after another couple of hours to the sounds of laughter and tears.

As Gemma and I arrive, last, the crowd erupts in cheers and applause. Gemma's mom and dad run to greet her. She dismounts and embraces her parents in a group hug. All three are crying happy tears.

Orien, Warren, Tina, Marcus, and Miranda all come to greet me. We shake hands, hug, and exchange compliments with each other. A few minutes later Gemma walks over with her mom and dad.

"James, this is my father, Erik."

"Dad, this is Prince James Edmonds."

"Your Highness, it is indeed an honor to meet you, and I am forever in your debt for what you have done for my Gemma. I have been informed about all that you did rescuing her."

Gemma gives me a hug. Her dad turns to Madeline and just raises an eyebrow.

"Yes dear, our daughter is courting the Prince. We'll talk later." Madeline chuckles back at Erik.

"We did again James, we brought our men back," says Gemma.

I give her a tight hug and hold her hand as we walk to the old tree stump. I stand on the stump and look around as everyone goes silent.

I begin... "Everyone! Where do I start? First, to the men, welcome home." Everyone goes wild yelling and clapping. "Everyone has put in so much work for us to arrive at this night. Men, you can be proud of your wives, daughters, sisters and mothers, they are remarkable women who have worked hard to aid in your rescue. This night we not only reunited this community, but we made it clear to Alazaar that we are a force to be reckoned with, and we will not stand down. Tonight, we let him know he is not untouchable." Again, there is cheers and applause.

"But also tonight, three of our members paid the ultimate price for our freedom. Three lives have been taken from us, and we will mourn with those families. Their loss is our loss, and we are here for you and with you. We will remember our fallen heroes and build a monument to their bravery."

"But we mustn't let their loss override the joy and celebration of this magnificent evening. Our beloved died so that we could take our Kingdom back, and that is nothing to be modest about. We honor them with the joy of Victory!" I scream, as joyous applause erupts.

"There's food and beer for everyone thanks to many women that stayed here today," shouts Katherine.

"Please, everyone, eat, drink, and celebrate," I say.

I step down and take Gemma's hands in mine. We just look at each other, and she leans in and kisses me in full view of everyone. My heart melts.

"Come, let us visit the injured and pay our respects to the dead."

Gemma's parents, and a few others gather round us. Erik extends his hand once more to shake. "Very well said Your Highness." Turning to Gemma he says, "We are so proud of you. When I was captured a few short weeks ago, you were but a girl. Now I see a full-grown woman, brave, strong, and beautiful. Thank you again Prince James for what you have done for this community, and for my family."

"I am humbled, and if not for your daughter's courage, I fear none of this would have transpired. She is indeed amazing."

"Mom, dad, go inside and eat. Especially you dad, you deserve a delicious meal. James and I are going to visit the injured and pay our respects, then we will be in."

Gemma and I leave and head to the makeshift hospital area in the cavern.

"She calls him James?" Erik asks Madeline.

"Per the Prince's request," Madeline replies, chuckling while taking her husband's hand to lead him to food.

There are about a dozen wounded men from the Mine, and a few injuries from the events of the evening. We greet every one of them and thank them for their sacrifice. Then we arrive at the morgue area with the families of the fallen nearby. We embrace them and offer condolences. Gemma breaks down and cries knowing all three of them well. I simply hold her.

"We will not forget," I tell the families.

"Thank you both for what you have done for our community. My husband died with a sword in his hand, fighting for us. We shall miss him, but we are also so proud of him," says one of the women.

"As well you should be," I reply.

Gemma and I leave and make our way to the cave. Her parents are sitting at a smaller table off to the side, so we join them. We are both very hungry and have a beer as well. We all chit chat about the events of the last few weeks, filling in her dad with missed details.

I speak up, "When my wife and daughter were murdered, I thought my life was over. Then when my father was exiled, I thought I would be killed. Yet because of the strength of your remarkable beautiful daughter, an entire community is whole again, and my heart has healed. I am truly grateful to know your daughter."

"Your Highness, you have been through much, and I know I am not your father. But, as a father, I can tell you the King would be so very proud of who you are."

Gemma smiles and squeezes her dad's hand, grateful for his acceptance of me as a good man.

"Thank you, Erik. That really means a lot."

After we eat Gemma and I look at each other and giggle, "A walk by the river?" I ask.

"Why yes my Prince, how did you know?" she laughs, and we head to the door.

We take leave of her parents and head down by the river. The air is cool, and the stars are shining brightly. The ground is lit well tonight by the moonlight, making it easier to walk the path. Once by the river she asks, "Well, all your plans worked. We did it. How do you feel?"

"Grateful. I feel incredibly grateful. For everything. But mostly for you. You have brought meaning and purpose back into my life."

Gemma blushes and smiles. "Me too James. I have never been so happy." She stops, and looking at me, she takes my hand.

"I am in love with you." I blurt out. "I love you."

Gemma wraps her arms around me, and our lips meet again. The passion rises as we melt into each other once more, and we hold each other so tight as our tongues dance together once more.

We break the kiss and just stare into each other's eyes.

"I love you too, James."

Chapter SIX: Alazaar's Revenge

Soldier's Arrive

The next few days bring smiles and laughter and lots of love everywhere once more. The men are excited to be back with their loved ones and involved with rebuilding within the cavern.

We also take time to bury and mourn the dead. Six dead in the village and three from the rescue at the Mine is a lot for such a small community.

The steering committee is reunited and begin to discuss future plans. This time as part of the Kingdom rather than just 'in' the Kingdom. They are all grateful for my part in reuniting the community, and they look to me to provide some insight into how we all work better together for the benefit of all.

Gemma returns to making wood shavings by day, while she and I form a deeper relationship in the evenings. Her father, Erik, is a good man and a leader in the community, so it's easy to see where Gemma gets her boldness.

We all know there will be repercussions because of what happened at the mine. Alazaar is sure to be furious, so we've sent scouts to Artems to keep watch and listen, but so far it has been quiet.

We have a meeting scheduled later today with Orien, Warren, Erik, Miranda, and others to discuss the layout of homes in the cavern as well as making a second entrance.

Gemma comes to find me, and she puts her arm around me. "Hello my Prince. What are you working on?" she asks.

"I am contemplating my alibi when I return to Artems. I said no going back, but I must try now to rescue my father. Ivan and Mark would both vouch that I left town for several days and thus had nothing to do with the mine."

"That's fine, but I'm not wearing that collar again," she says.

"Agreed. No, my dear, you shall not ever wear that collar again. But I must return and talk with others about next steps and my father."

Gemma leans down and kisses me gently, "I understand, and we are all here for you James. Now I'm going to help my mom with some chores. I'll see you at supper."

"Okay, you be safe, and I'll be there."

"Alazaar's Soldier's, Alazaar's Soldier's. They're coming, They're coming. Move! Prince James, soldiers are coming!" A girl comes racing into the cave out of breath. It's Rachel, I recognize her. She runs to the table; breathing hard, she says to me. "Prince James, soldiers are coming, five of them, headed this way."

Rachel's frantic, and her screaming causes quite a commotion; others come running as well.

Orien arrives, "If they find us and live to report it, we're all dead Your Highness."

"Everyone, prepare for a fight. Safeguard the children. Orien, let's go." I get my sword.

Orien, Warren, Erik, and Gemma, all follow me. "Rachel, show us." Rachel runs back to her horse, and we all mount up and follow her. "Across the river," she charges, and we all follow.

We make fast time across the river, but slow our pace, as riders approach. We stand our ground, prepared to fight; the riders arrive. It's the same five from a couple of days ago. The leader speaks, "What is the meaning of this? I knew you were no merchant. Who are you?" he asks.

Gemma responds, "He is Prince James Edmonds. Have you no respect for the true crown?"

"Prince James? Your Highness," he says smugly. "Wait until Alazaar is made aware of your activities, out here with these rebels."

"And who do I have the pleasure of addressing may I ask?"

"I am Maximus Dreskonia, loyal servant to Alazaar, and I will take him your head on a stick, Your Highness."

"You may try, but you are five against a hundred, bring it on, today is your last day of service to your Alazaar. I will make sure he receives your burnt corpse."

With that Maximus pulls his horse to its hind legs and all five men charge. Ten more of our men and women come out of the woods, and the battle begins. Swords clash, and blood flows, as our members attack with long spears. Three adversaries fall quickly at the hands of Orien and those beside him.

As fate would have it, Gemma comes face to face with a towering man wielding a sword. "You're too pretty to kill but kill you I must." He charges Gemma, while swinging his sword, but Gemma is small, agile, and fast. She dodges his swing, but he connects with her mid-section. She screams in pain as blood flows across her side. The soldier spins for a second pass, as Erik thrusts his sword into the soldier's chest. The man falls to the ground, and Erik runs to his daughter. Gemma has a long gash across the left side of her abdomen. Tears flow as she holds her side, blood covering her hands.

Meanwhile I face off with Maximus, he swings and our swords clash; again, and again. All my years of practice come back instantly, and I defend myself from his attacks. Then in an instant I land a well-placed blow, and my sword slices open his neck. He falls to his knees, gasping as blood pours from his neck.

"Before you die, know this, there will be a place beside you in hell for your beloved Alazaar." I thrust my sword into his chest, and he drops.

I run to Gemma. "Gemma, my Gemma."

Erik has her in his arms, "She will be okay, but she needs medical attention quickly. We must get her to Clara, fast."

I jump on my horse and say to Erik, "hand her to me. Then, please clean up here. Thank you all."

Erik lifts Gemma up to me on my horse and I hold her side saddle as she rests in my arms. I pull the reins and race back to the cave.

"Clara! Madeline! Come quickly!" The ladies emerge from the cave and see me holding Gemma, blood down the front of her.

"Gemma!" Madeline screams as the ladies and two others help me lower her down to them. I jump down and take her back into my arms. She wraps her arms around my neck, and we race to a bed in the medical area. There Clara takes charge. As I lay her down, Gemma grasps my hand in hers.

"Don't leave me James," she says.

"I'm right here by your side, I'm not leaving you." She faints; probably from loss of blood and fatigue, but I squeeze her hand in mine.

Clara immediately begins to work on her, cleaning and stitching the wound. "She'll be okay Your Highness. She's lost a lot of blood and just needs to rest. She's lucky, the wound is not deep and none of her internal organs were damaged."

I hold her hand in one hand and run my fingers through her hair and down her face with the other just caressing her as Madeline cries. I don't leave her side for hours.

Eventually Erik says, "Your Highness, you must eat. Go and eat. We will stay with her."

Miranda and Katherine both tug at my arms to come and eat. I get up, not wanting to take my eyes off Gemma, but reluctantly make my way to the main table. As I arrive there, I see Rachel to the side. I walk to her, pull her into my embrace, and whisper. "You saved us Rachel. You saved us all."

I turn to those present, "Here is our hero today. This fast-thinking, fast riding young girl deserves all our gratitude. She saved us all." Everyone stands, applauding and cheering for Rachel.

"How old are you?" I ask her.

"I am seventeen years of age Your Highness."

"Only seventeen, such uncredible courage. Where are your parents?"

"We are here Your Highness. I am Klinten, this is my wife, Anna."

"Greetings to you both. Be very proud of this young lady," I say as I pull her close to me once more, with my arm around her. "She truly is the hero today."

"Thank you, Your Highness, we are honored," he replies.

Rachel smiles and blushes and hugs her mom.

I sit to eat some food Katherine prepared for me. Orien sits down and just looks at me. "How are you?" I ask.

"Your Highness. Your swordsmanship against Maximus was amazing. Where did you learn to fight like that," he asks.

"It was part of my studies as a young man. Years of playing with swords against fake enemies in my father's court. I never thought anything of it until today. I was so angry at Maximus; my training just took over."

"Indeed, Your Highness. We buried those men. All of them. I trust that remark about sending his corpse back to Alazaar was only tough talk. It's best to not let Alazaar know about his loss today just yet."

"Yes, Orien, incredibly wise of you. Thank you. You and Erik also displayed some amazing fighting skills today as well. Very nicely done."

"Thank you. It's been a long time since I raised a sword against another man. But it had to be done."

"Indeed, it did my friend. Indeed it did. And, will need to be done many times again I fear before this fight is over."

Clara comes in and up to the table, "Gemma is awake and asking for you, Your Highness."

I leap from the table. "How is she?"

"She is fine, just weak and tired, but she asked for you."

"Yes. Thank you, Clara." I race back to where Gemma lay. She has a few pillows under her head, her abdomen wrapped in bandages. Her eyes are open, and she is talking to people.

I walk to her side, take her hand in mine once more and begin kissing her fingers. "Oh Gemma. Thank the heavens you are okay."

"Hello James. She starts giggling, quietly. You lied to me. You can fight! I saw you use your sword today. That man was huge, yet you defeated him with little effort; my Prince."

I lean in and gently kiss her on the lips. "You did well today also, but you scared me badly. I have been so worried."

"I'll be fine James. But I want to learn to fight like you. Will you teach me to fight?"

"Let's not concern ourselves with that right now. Promise me you will get well, then we can talk about what's next."

"Okay James. I love you."

"I love you too, dear Gemma."

Clara speaks up, "Okay she needs her rest. Let her be. Prince James, a couple of men moved your cot here to remain near Gemma." Gemma smiles knowing I will be close.

I kiss her again and stand to meet Erik and Madeline. "Thank you, Erik, for saving her today. I have lost two women I loved; I cannot lose another."

"Your Highness, she is my daughter, I would give my life for hers any day."

We embrace each other and walk around to my cot. This afternoon events were certainly unexpected, and I wonder how often we must face such men, and whether we will be as lucky in victory next time. I lay down and reach for Gemma's hand, then close my eyes and relax, feeling comfortable being so close to her. I fall asleep quickly.

Returning to Work

The next morning, I wake up and my eyes focus on Gemma laying next to me. She's still asleep and so peaceful. I reach for her hand again and kiss her fingers. She senses my kisses and opens her eyes.

"Good morning my dear," I say.

She smiles and looks at me through groggy eyes. She winces, clearly in pain.

"Are you okay, can I get you anything?" I ask. She is clearly in pain.

"My side hurts badly."

I get up and find Clara who comes to check on Gemma.

Clara removes her bandages too check on her wound. "Good morning Gemma. Well, you certainly have a very nasty gash as I said yesterday. But everything looks as good as can be expected; you're very lucky that sword didn't go much deeper. I believe you will be fine, but I'm not surprised that you're in pain. I'll get you some herbs, but you are going to hurt for few days."

Gemma thanks Clara as Clara applies new bandages and hands her herbal tea to kill the pain. Afterward Gemma lays on her right side, facing me.

"I can't believe I let that man get me," she says.

"You're lucky you weren't killed. Had your father not been there..."

She knows she messed up, so I don't want to make it worse by scolding her, but I feel I must let her know how concerned I was - am.

"I do admire your courage Gemma, and we will take back our Kingdom eventually together, but I can't lose you. When my wife and daughter were killed, I nearly gave up on life. You've brought me back from that. I won't survive losing you."

I kiss the back of her hand hoping to express my concern and love for her.

"I know," she says. "That was stupid and selfish of me. I didn't even consider what it would do to you or my father if I was struck by a fatal blow. I'm sorry James."

"He didn't kill you because you're very fast and agile. You did good in protecting yourself. And I forgive you of course, but we will get you some real training. In fact, I was actually thinking about that recently. Perhaps Alexandra would make a better teacher for you than I. My ways take years to master, and we don't have years. Plus, I've never taught anybody."

"Oh, Yes James, I would love to learn with Alexandra. Do you think she would come here?"

"Probably not, but I need to visit the King of Westerly and speak with him regarding the events in our Kingdom. Perhaps in a few days when you are well, we could travel to Westerly together. How does that sound?"

"Really? You would take me to Westerly with you? I would love to go. And I will work hard to learn." She caresses my face with her hand, still not wanting to move much although the tea is helping kill the pain.

"Very well, I will speak with your parents."

"Thank you James. I do love you."

"I love you too. Now you rest. I'm going to get coffee and meet with Orien and Warren." I lean over and kiss her lips once more. She embraces the kiss and smiles at me.

I head for coffee at the usual place, and Katherine has coffee waiting. "How is Gemma Your Highness?" she asks.

"She is fighting the pain, but she's strong and will be fine."

Katherine replies, "praise the heavens she wasn't killed."

"Indeed."

I speak with Orien and Warren regarding the activities of the day, we go to visit the cavern, which is where most of the activity is taking place.

As we arrive at the cavern Ryan greets us. "Come, let me show you our plans for a back entrance." We walk to the west side of the cavern, and he shows us how the rocks in the wall are already breaking apart. On the other side of this area is flat ground that will allow for lumber staging.

He says, "We've been talking, and we think we should return to the mine and liberate them from some of that rail track and a few cars. We could retrofit the cars into flat cars, and the lumber could roll through the cavern until it is properly sized and ready for delivery."

"You want to return to the mine and steal rail and cars?" Warren asks.

"I love it!" I say. "With planning, we can do that. The mine will take weeks to be back in operation with the miners gone, and another defeat against Alazaar would drive him insane."

Ryan smiles, Orien laughs and then says, "It is a daring plan, and has substantial dangers, but that is the life we face now. We could make it work Your Highness, and adding rail to our operation would greatly enhance our profits."

"Very well then, let's start planning. Excellent idea Ryan."

We turn our attention to other details of the cavern layout and how homes could be built closer to the passageway, on the southeast side. Everyone has put a lot of thought into it, and with the men back, it can come together quickly.

I then head down by the river: Madeline, Erik, and others are baiting fish traps for fresh food. "Erik, may I speak with you when you are free?"

"Of course, Your Highness, I'll be right there."

"Good morning, Prince James." yells Madeline.

Erik makes his way out of the water and heads toward me, wiping fish bait off his hands as he does so. "Good morning Your Highness, how is our Gemma?"

"Gemma is good. Clara is still saying she will be fine, but she's going to need several days to recover. I say it again, thank the heavens you were there."

"She's a brave girl and I'm proud of her, but she doesn't always think before she leaps, Your Highness."

"She is young, and inexperienced, but she is smart and fast. Which brings me to why I am here. You know I am very much in love with your daughter."

Erik cuts me off, "Yes Your Highness and apparently she with you," he says with as big a smile he can muster.

"She needs training. Real training, training that I cannot give her. I need to go to Westerly to visit the King, and I wish to take Gemma with me, when she's well enough of course, to train with Alexandra. There she could learn much more quickly than here, plus Gemma and Alexandra seem to have developed a friendship while Alexandra was here."

"But I would never take her without your permission sir."

Erik sits on a rock and takes a deep breath. "I always knew that girl was destined for adventure. Ever since she was just four years old, she'd run off into the woods and return with stories of defeating an army. She's a dreamer, that one, but her mother and I are so very proud of her."

"I can't imagine a more fitting way for Gemma to learn to defend herself than traveling with you, Your Highness. It would be an honor for our family for her to do so."

"Yes, Your Highness, you have my permission. When she's well."

"Of course. Thank you, Erik, I will make sure she is safe, and we will stay maybe two months."

He stands up and shakes my hand. "You're a good man Prince James. I could ask no better a man for my daughter."

"Thank you, Erik. I will take care of her. Now how about we finish those fish traps?"

"It's a fine morning to do just that. Madeline, do you need more bait?" he yells.

"Yes dear, perhaps two more handfuls."

We start back to work.

By mid-afternoon we're done and have enough fish to feed us all for several days.

I return to check on Gemma who is peacefully sleeping. I sit on the cot next to her, but she hears me and opens her eyes. She's groggy from that herbal tea earlier, but she doesn't appear to be in pain.

"Hello my darling. How are you feeling?" I ask.

"I'm okay. just very tired. What did Clara put in my tea?"

"I'm sure a strong pain killer to help you rest. It's going to be a couple days before you're back on your feet my love." I brush her hair, and just admire her beauty.

"I'm hungry," she says.

"Hungry? We can fix that, let me go find Katherine."

Katherine is more than happy to rustle up some simple food for Gemma and assists her as she eats it. Gemma is appreciative and lays back to rest.

The next couple of days are about the same, except Gemma gets a little more strength each day. By day three she is standing up. I have my arm around her as we make our way to the kitchen area, offering her some steadiness as she walks, still weak from the ordeal.

Those in the room clap as Gemma makes her entrance. She blushes and waves to everyone. Several come to greet her and welcome her back among us.

By day four, she's walking on her own.

I see Gemma come toward the central table, walking on her own. "Looks who's up."

"Good morning," she says as she makes her way to me. She leans down and kisses me.

"How are you feeling? Want coffee?" I ask.

"I feel good, just about back to my old self, and I would love coffee." She sits down as I get up to get her a cup of coffee. Katherine is out at the moment, I'm not really sure where she headed this morning. I pour Gemma coffee and sit next to her taking her hand in mine. "It's so nice to have you back moving around."

"Oh gosh yes. I am so tired of laying on that cot. I got a couple hours exercise yesterday, but I'm going to try and stay busy today."

"Well just be careful not to overdo it."

She asks if she missed anything, and I tell her about the plans Ryan and the men have for another entrance and the thoughts about using rail.

She laughs, "Oh won't that really grate Alazaar, stealing his rail system. I love it, when are we going to do that?" she asks.

"I doubt you're ready for a trip like that anytime soon, but they want to cut the entrance first so no hurry."

A few minutes later Erick and Madeline come over.

Erik asks, "So did you tell her about her big upcoming trip?"

Gemma replies, "to steal the rail? I heard."

"Oh no dear, not that. About your training?" he asks.

Gemma looks at me quizzically.

"I asked your dad about you accompanying me to Westerly, so you could work and learn with Alexandra."

Gemma lights up. "You did?" She looks at her father. "And you and mom are okay with it?" She claps her hands and makes her way around the table to hug her mom and dad. "Thank you both. I will be extra careful, and I'll do as James asks the whole time. Oh, Thank you."

Madeline speaks up. "You're a grown woman now Gemma, you don't need our permission anymore. And you've proven yourself to be responsible. We are so proud of you, and we believe the training Alexandra will provide will be good for you, and for our community."

Gemma gets so exited she bounces.

"Careful there, don't pull your wound back open," says Erik.

She hugs her dad again, kisses him on the cheek, and returns to sit by me. "So, when do we leave, James?"

"I'm thinking about the first part of next week. How does that sound?"

"That sounds wonderful. I am so excited."

I chuckle at her excitement. "After the last few days, it's good to see you to be happy again. You deserve it."

"Yes, thank you, and thanks for asking my dad for permission. That was very gentlemanly of you." She kisses me again, and I never get tired of that.

We finish our coffee and walk outside to the river, just because she hasn't been out of the cave in days. I hold her hand as we walk.

"Oh, it is so good to be out of that cave," she says. "I have learned my lesson James, and I promise to be so much more careful going forward."

I stop and pull her close. "I've missed holding you in my arms," I look into her amazing, beautiful eyes once more, as they sparkle in the sunlight.

"Mmmm, I've missed being in your arms, my Prince."

124

Our mouths melt together once more as we embrace each other. We take it easy the rest of the morning and into the afternoon, just walking in the woods, checking in with community members, and visiting the cavern.

The Guillotine

Around mid-afternoon a rider from the community comes in asking for me. "Where is Prince James, I must speak with him."

Gemma and I are back at the central table chatting with folks as he makes his way to us. "Prince James, I have important news from the city."

"Yes, please tell us about the city, what is Alazaar up to now?"

"Alazaar is threatening violence Your Highness. He has called for a town meeting in the castle square in two days' time. He is furious about the escape of the men at the mine, and the rescue of the captured women. He has declared those responsible will be found and executed. He's even rolled out the guillotine Your Highness. He claims he will demonstrate its use at the town meeting."

"Well, we knew this day was coming. I guess we shall go to town in two days' time and see what evil Alazaar has planned this time. What about it Gemma, you up for a trip back to Artems?"

"Absolutely James. We need to hear his plans so we can form our own. And after I am better trained, we will destroy his evil reign."

Orien overhearing the conversation says. "I'm coming with you as well."

"Me also," says Erik.

"Very well, as always, I thank you and welcome your support."

The next day Gemma gets even stronger and returns to doing light work around the community. Her love for the people and eagerness to help anyone is exemplary.

The following morning, we prepare for Artems. We don't plan to enter the castle for fear of being seen, but we will have an unobstructed view from nearby rooftops that I know Mark can help us reach. I am worried about what type of stunt Alazaar has planned. He is truly evil and cares not about anyone. I feel sick at the thought that others will pay the price for what we have done.

Gemma can sense I am concerned and offers her affection, which I cherish, but I also don't wish to worry her. We walk out to the horses and meet up with Orien and Erik.

"Good morning Your Highness. Are you ready for today," asks Erik.

"I'm as ready as I'll be. And we will do what we must."

"Indeed, we will James."

That's the first time he has ever called me James. And it means a lot, today of all days, that he expressed his closeness and concern for me in such a simple gesture. I nod in reply.

"And how about my beautiful daughter? Is your dad going to have to save you again?" he asks laughing.

"No father, surely, we won't do any fighting today. I suspect Alazaar has his whole army surrounding the castle."

We all mount up and head out. We can go at a faster pace today, with everyone on horses and a deadline to meet. Alazaar set his demonstration for two-o'clock pm.

The journey is somber, but it's a beautiful day. We all talk about the work going on by the men in the cavern and how fast everything is coming

126

together. Orien jokes about some of the silly things some of the men have done in moments of carelessness. Everything from being hit by a hammer to pulling the roof off one of the buildings because someone forgot to unhitch the horses. Gemma laughs loud and long over that one. In spite of all that's happened, spirits are still high, and optimism is everywhere.

We arrive in Artems and make our way to the market to find Mark. He's in the tavern as usual. He spots us and points upstairs rather than saying anything out loud. We make our way up the backstairs and into the small room again where we can talk.

"James, it's so good to see you again my friend. Come to see what devilish activity Alazaar has in store for us I assume?"

He then greets Orien and Gemma, welcoming them back, and meets Erik."

"Ah Erik, what a lovely and brave daughter you have. You must be immensely proud. And she's so beautiful as well."

"We are indeed."

Gemma hugs Mark. "Hello Mark, good to see you again."

Mark points out the second-floor window toward the castle. "Come, if we go this way, we can stay above the crowd and get close enough to see and hear everything."

We all follow Mark out the window and make our way across the market rooftops towards the castle wall. As we get closer, we can hear the crowd get louder and louder. Finally, we arrive at a place where we have good visibility of the courtyard, while still remaining somewhat obscured from view by higher buildings and other people.

The guillotine is an exceptionally large machine that moves on six wheels. It has a flat platform on top that could easily hold twenty men.

The blade raises at least another ten feet in the air, and when released delivers a swift and cutting blow. The wooden bench where the victim is laid is covered with blood stains from times past. But this machine has not been used in decades, at least not while my father has been upon the throne. Alazaar has clearly rebuilt it for new use.

Gemma lies next to me for a better view. The courtyard easily holds a thousand people, and it is packed. It is ten minutes until 2:00pm. Guards march out of the castle's ground level floor and surround the guillotine. A few minutes later, Alazaar's generals and diplomats appear, walking up the steps, and taking their place on the platform. Without further a due, Alazaar makes his grand entrance.

Dressed in full military armor, and wielding his sword and shield, his shield displaying the Kingdom's Coat of Arms. Gemma gasps as she sees him. Alazaar moves to the front of the platform to speak. He is a very large, very muscular man. He is clean shaven but has little hair atop his head. On his face is a horrible scar down the left side. He is - ugly.

Stretching out his arms, he begins to speak.

"People of Artems, welcome to your Castle. When I came to power, I came to offer peace and prosperity for all in our Kingdom. And my soldiers work to maintain peace and order. People live within the laws we have established, and we have welcomed trade from faraway places."

The crowd dares not say anything for fear of death. The silence is deafening.

"My people. Recently, a series of violent crimes have taken place within our city. Our women were stolen from their places of work. And our men at the mine were taken against their will."

Gemma whispers, anger in her eyes, "He is such a liar."

128

"My people, these acts of violence have not gone unnoticed and will not go unpunished. Therefore, I have resurrected our instrument of punishment. This fine machine on which I stand, stands as a monument to order and justice."

"My people. I know these crimes have not been conducted by members of our great city, but by cowards living in the forests of our Kingdom. They hide, likes moles, unwilling to show their faces during sunlit hours. But we will find these moles, and we will crush these rebels. What they stand for is the old order. The order of weak men. Men who would rather talk then take what is theirs by strength. And today I give you the leader of these men."

He stretched out his hand, and from the dark shadows of the castle, comes forth a man escorted by guards, bound in chains, his head covered, he is lead up the stairs. The man is paraded before all and delivered to Alazaar.

"Today my people, today I give you, their leader."

He pulls the cover from the man's head.

"Today, I give you King Phillip Edmonds."

The crowd goes wild as they see there King stand before them. He was long assumed dead.

Gemma grasps my hand, "James, your father. He's alive."

I swallow hard at the site of my father chained and bound by Alazaar.

"People here me," continues Alazaar. "Here before you stands the man you once called King. Here is the man who inspires these rebels in our Kingdom to attack us. But we will stand for it no longer. Guards!"

At once the Guards move into action. They pick up my father and lay him on the bed of the guillotine. My father makes no motion of fight.

"People, today ends the old rule and the end of this rebel leader."

I shudder as I realize what's about to happen. My father is placed in the correct position for his execution. Gemma's grip on my arm tightens.

Alazaar orders, "Guards, pull."

At once a Guard pulls the lever releasing the blade. It falls fast and true, and my father's head falls into the basket beneath in a split second. Fresh blood runs down the front of the device.

The crowd cries out. Gemma buries her face in my side and weeps silently. I watch in disbelief what I just witnessed. Tears fall down my face.

"People of Artems. Let this be a sign. The old Kingdom is dead. I am your King, and you will pay me homage or face the same fate. We must root out these evil rebels who seek to destroy our Kingdom. And we will. Good day my beloved subjects. Your King has spoken."

He turns and walks back, returning to the castle, followed by the Generals and Diplomats. The guards push the large machine back inside the castle overhang.

My father's body still lays atop the machine.

The crowd begins to break apart. We stand in silence and move back quickly to the room at Mark's tavern. Once inside Gemma hugs me firmly and cries hard. I hold her tightly, as my shoulder becomes wet from her tears.

"James, we extend our deepest sorrows to you. Your father was a good man, and we will avenge his death," says Erik.

I nod, still holding to Gemma tightly.

Mark speaks, "James, in my wildest nightmares...I am so sorry my friend. We are here for you."

"Thank you. My friends. My Gemma. Come, we must retreat back to the cave before I place you all in danger."

I hug Mark goodbye, and we make our way to the horses.

"Where is Orien," I ask.

"He has ridden ahead Your Highness, to alert the people as to what has happened," Erik replies.

Gemma, Erik, and I take our leave and begin the journey back. No one says anything all the way home.

Once we arrive at the cave, everyone is outside, waiting for our return. Orien has informed everyone regarding my father's execution. Madeline and Katherine are the first to greet us.

"Your Highness, we have heard the horribly news and we all offer our love and support to you," says Katherine.

Gemma leaps from her horse and runs into her mother's arms. Orien, and the others come, offering their condolences. I make my way to the tree stump and stand to speak.

"My friends. My family. Today our Kingdom suffered a brutal loss at the hands of evil. Today we lost a good man, one of our own, one who loved you all. One who loved me. I had the honor and privilege to call him father, and he was a fine father. I will surely miss him. I thank you all for everything you have done for me. For your Love, and for entrusting me with your Gemma."

The crowd claps as I step down. As I get my bearings, Gemma stands upon the tree stump. "Everyone, everyone, I wish to speak." The crowd goes silent as Gemma looks at me.

"James, Your Highness, today I witnessed what true evil looks like. When I met you, I feared you also to be evil. Little did I know how much you would teach me about what goodness really is. You have given all of yourself to me, to all of us. You have given us hope, and courage, and strength to fight for what is ours, and we shall never forget that. To me personally, you have shown me what real love looks like as well."

She stops to collect herself, wiping away her tears.

"Today, James, you paid the ultimate sacrifice as you laid with us and watched your father's execution. People of Timbervale, hear me. King Phillip Edmonds is dead. But out of the sorrow, James, you have been elevated. My family and my friends, I present to you all our new King, King James Edmonds."

The crowd claps and yells joyous words. Someone yells out, "Long live the King." And the crowd responds in unison. "Long live the King!"

"The throne is yours now James, you are our King, and we are your loving and loyal subjects." Gemma steps down and comes before me. Going to her knees she recites. "James, from this day forward, you are no longer Your Highness. From this day forward you are and will forever be: Your Majesty. And I pledge my life to you."

The whole crowd goes to their knees reciting, "Your Majesty, we pledge our lives to you."

I take Gemma by her hands and lift her up. "If I am to be your King, then I shall require a Queen." I fall to one knee, while holding Gemma's hand. "My dear Gemma, I believed I could never love again. Then I met you, and my life changed. My heart leaps when I'm in your presence. All of me is in love with all of you. And so, with your Father's blessing, dearest Gemma, will you become my Queen? Will you marry me and take me as your humble husband?"

Gemma begins to cry and looks to her father, waiting for his approval.

It takes a few moments and a pinch from Madeline for Erik to grasp what is happening, but he steps forward saying, "Oh yes, yes of course, my daughter you have my approval and my blessing." he says.

Gemma looks at me, her eyes wide, her smile beaming, tears flowing down her face. "Yes, Your Majesty, I will be your Queen. And yes, James, I will take you as my husband and I shall be your wife."

Everyone cheers, and Gemma and I fall into each other's arms, our lips melt together again, our tongues dance, and bodies form tightly together. Madeline is crying, most others are too. Erik comes up to congratulate both of us.

"May a humble old man hug his future Queen?" he asks Gemma.

Gemma hugs her dad. "Father, I'm still your daughter."

"True, but until a few minutes ago you were only my daughter. Now you are to be my Queen, Your Royal Highness."

Gemma sheds more tears of happiness and collapses into her father's arms. Madeline comes over and joins the embrace. Others follow, greeting the new Princess of the Kingdom with her proper title. "Your Royal Highness"

After lots of tears, both of sorrow and joy, the crowd breaks up. Gemma looks at me, "Well Your Majesty, would you like to take a walk with your to-be queen?"

We walk to the river and sit in the sand. The moon casts enough light to make shadows. I look at Gemma and our lips meet once again. As I break the kiss, I finally let go of my emotions.

I lie there, nestled in Gemma's arms, and I cry.

Chapter SEVEN: Times Past

Jealousies Form

.... many years earlier

The girls loved to play in the shallow creek, trying to catch fish with their bare hands. They would giggle and splash and pretend all sorts of adventures as all young children do. They were the best of friends.

Maria and Morena were eight years old and have lived next to each other in Artems their whole lives. Maria, with her curly blond hair, and Morena with long black hair being their only difference.

They would run, study, work, and eat together and this day was no different. They were pretending to host a tea party in the castle for all the women of the Kingdom.

"Come on Morena, we must make sure everything is ready for all the ladies when they arrive. Everything must be perfect. This is the castle after all," claims Maria.

Morena replies, "Why yes Maria, everything must look perfect. Won't our husbands be so proud of us, Maria? We can show them that women are capable of more than just fixing them meals."

"Oh Morena, but I want to cook for my husband when I am grown. And I want to dance in big ball rooms with him and hold his hand as we walk through the forest," says Maria. "I want to look in his eyes and feel loved."

"You're such a romantic Maria. I'm going to use magic to give my husband everything he wants so he knows how much I love him," she replies.

The girls giggle and complete their mission setting up make believe teacups for all.

"Hi Maria, hi Morena." Alazaar, their senior by two years, comes and asks what they're doing.

Morena wastes no time. "Hello Alazaar, come and sit my prince and have a cup of tea." Morena displays her affection for Alazaar every chance she gets, even at so young an age, which embarrasses Alazaar completely.

"A cup of tea? Men don't drink tea Morena, we drink beer and ale. Silly girl," says Alazaar.

He continues, "we've just come in from fishing and we captured baskets full. I want to share it all with you Maria. Will you dine with me?" he asks, extending his hand to Maria.

Morena offers to eat with Alazaar, but it is evident Alazaar is infatuated with Maria. Maria thanks him but passes on the offer not to upset Morena.

Time passes, Maria and Morena grow into beautiful teenage girls, attracting the attention of many of the young men in Artems. But Morena maintains her affection for Alazaar. Unfortunately, Alazaar does not return her feelings. He is still infatuated with Maria. Approaching her one evening, he says, "Maria, there is a dance in two days at the castle. I would be honored if you would allow me to be your escort for the evening."

Maria looks to Morena, knowing how she feels, but what can she say? If she turns down Alazaar's request, there is no certainty he would then ask Morena, it is clear he has never been attracted to her. And, she may

135

not have anyone else in their community offer to escort her to the ball. She thinks for a few minutes.

"Why Alazaar, I would be happy to attend the dance with you. How kind of you to ask," she responds.

Morena is crushed that her best friend is going to the dance with Alazaar. Even if he did ask her, she knows Maria understands how she feels about Alazaar. But, they've been friends forever, so she lets it go.

"I hope you enjoy the dance, Maria. I'm jealous, but it should be a great time, so I'm happy for you."

"Thanks, Morena. I know how you feel about Alazaar, but I couldn't turn him down. He was so sweet to ask me. Please don't be upset with me."

"I completely understand, but I'm still jealous," she says laughing.

Two days pass quickly, and Maria is excited to attend the ball. She's never been inside the castle before and is eager to meet the quests and dignitaries. Alazaar meets her with a carriage he borrowed from friends of the family, and the two ride happily to the castle.

Morena sits at home and sulks. She wants to be happy for Maria, but she's having a hard time letting this go. Her feelings for Alazaar are strong and she wants him for herself. She feels betrayed by Maria.

Maria and Alazaar enter the grand ballroom like royalty. It's immense size, and the ornate decor is more beautiful than anything she has ever seen. Alazaar feels a sense of pride that he has been able to impress Maria. He has fallen for Maria, not caring about Morena's feelings for him.

The two make their way around the room, greeting guests, being introduced, and enjoy being some of the youngest in the room at eighteen years of age. The music starts and Alazaar escorts Maria to the dance floor.

Dancing is common in their community on weekend evenings, and Maria loves to dance. She feels like a princess and doesn't want the night to end. The splendor and majesty of it all is so romantic.

A short while later, trumpets sound, and the room falls silent. A gentleman at the stairs announces the arrival of the royal family. King Germaine Edmonds, Queen Victoria, and Prince Phillip. They walk down the grand staircase with such elegance and poise, Maria is captivated. As the King and Queen begin chatting with guests, the music restarts and everyone returns to dance.

Alazaar is polite and a perfect gentleman. He is also a very good dancer. Maria is impressed. She has always seen Alazaar as the local bully enforcing his way on the other kids in the neighborhood. But tonight, he is a much gentler, much kinder, young man.

As the evening progresses, the King and Queen make their rounds and arrive at the group with Maria and Alazaar. The King comments, "how nice it is to see so many young couples here from our Kingdom tonight. We are complimented that have joined us tonight in our celebration."

Maria curtsies, "Your Majesty."

Alazaar bows properly, showing his respect. Behind the King is Prince Phillip. He steps forward and takes Maria's hand, attracted instantly to her charm.

"May I inquire as to the name of this lovely young lady?"

Alazaar responds, "Your Highness, may I introduce Maria Alexander."

"What an enchanting young lady you are. Would it be rude of me to show you around the castle? Good sir, do you mind?" he asks of Alazaar.

Maria looks at Alazaar, not quite sure how to respond.

Alazaar responds, "She would love to Your Highness," relieving Maria of the embarrassment of saying no, feeling an obligation to Alazaar as her escort.

Maria nods and thanks Alazaar for his kindness. She has never danced with anyone outside the neighborhood before, and never dreamed of having a dance with the Prince.

"Thank you Alazaar, that's very kind of you," says the Prince as he continues to hold Maria's hand. He leads her away from the ballroom and to the courtyard. There he begins to show her various elements of the castle grounds and educates her about some of the history of the castle.

Maria feels she has been transported into a fairytale. The night is warm, and the moon casts a warm glow over the castle grounds. She's not so much interested in what the Prince is saying, and she is just delighted to be here with him.

The Prince is extremely handsome, twenty years of age, polite, and kind. They walk together and she tries to pay attention to what he shows her and tells her.

"So, Maria, I've gone on and on about the castle. Forgive me if I've bored you. Do tell me about you," he suggests.

"There's not much to tell Your Highness. I was born and raised here in Artems. My father works as a blacksmith, tending mostly to the needs of horses. My mother teaches us and tends to our needs. We all have chores and help with whatever we need done. We live a simple life, but I would like very much to hear about you, Your Highness. Not as much about the castle, but about what your life is like."

Prince Phillip explains what life is like in the castle, and how he sometimes feels tied down. He wishes he could get out more often to visit the people of the Kingdom, determining what their needs are, how the monarchy can help them, how to govern them. He goes on to talk about the affairs of the Kingdom, and what it takes to maintain order and peace. But his father feels that is the work of dignitaries, and not the role of a Prince.

Maria is impressed by his tales. They continue to walk, returning closer to the ballroom, they can hear the music playing.

"Would you like to dance?" he asks.

Maria simply nods as he takes her in his arms and they begin to waltz around the large patio, having the entire area to themselves. Maria gets lost in his eyes and the music, and forgets the world exists. If she were wearing glass slippers, she thinks to herself, 'I could pass for Cinderella.'

Time goes fast, and the ball comes to an end. The Prince escorts Maria back to central ballroom, returning her to Alazaar.

"Forgive me," he says. "I seem to have stolen her away from you for the evening. I do hope you both will return soon."

"Of course, Your Highness, we'd love too," Maria replies.

The Prince kisses her hand and bids her goodnight.

Maria returns her focus to Alazaar who escorts her home.

"Please do forgive me Alazaar, it was rude of me to allow the Prince to keep me for so long. Were you able to enjoy yourself?" she asks.

"Oh yes, I danced with some others and spoke with some of the other young men. There is much happening in the kingdom, and I want to be part of it, so it was nice to make contacts. You looked lovely dancing with the Prince."

"You saw that? I was nervous at first, but soon forgot where I was." The Prince is an exceptional dancer, but so are you Alazaar. It's been a lovely evening, and it was nice of the Prince to show and teach me things I may never see again. I'm really glad you had a good evening considering how it turned out.

Alazaar escorts Maria home, maintaining his pleasantness, but inside feels betrayed, even frustrated that the Prince would do such a thing.

Days turn into weeks and Maria's fairytale evening becomes a memory. She settles back to her studies and chores, and she and Morena forget the ball and remain friends.

Alazaar continues to show his affection toward her via compliments and flowers, leading to more hurt feelings for Morena, but she tries to remain happy for Maria.

Early the next morning, a commotion arises in the street. People gather to see what is gaining attention. Soon everyone is made aware the Prince is passing through town, returning from business elsewhere in the Kingdom. All want a chance to see and wave.

As he passes, he spots Maria, standing in common work cloths and dirty from the daily chores. He stops, and stares. "Maria? Is that you?" He dismounts his horse and approaches her. Even in dirty work clothes, Maria's blonde hair and charm shine through. "It is so good to see you. I have thought of you often since the ball."

Maria blushes, embarrassed at her attire. "Your Highness," she curtsies once more in front of him.

"It is fate that I have found you again. Please, introduce me to your parents and friends."

Maria complies with his request, but protests, "Your Highness, I am not properly dressed, not properly bathed, to greet you. Forgive me."

Prince Phillip laughs. "You are splendidly charming in your attire." He reaches up and removes a leaf from her hair. She blushes, totally embarrassed.

The Prince greets those nearby, and Maria's parents. "I am delighted to know now where you live. I would like to call on you again, with your father's permission of course."

Her father nods, smiling happily.

Maria blushes, "I would very much like that, Your Highness."

"Very well then, it's settled, I shall return tomorrow at this time, and we shall spend the evening together, if that is acceptable?"

Maria nods, "I shall look forward to it, Your Highness."

The Prince smiles and mounts his horse. A few minutes later, he is gone.

Everyone is amazed at what just happened. Morena jades Maria, "Maria, the Prince is enraptured with you."

Her mother chimes in as well, "Maria, what happened at the ball? You said you met the royal family. You said nothing about catching the eye of the Prince."

"Oh mother, we danced and talked."

"Well, you obviously made a very good impression. Prince or not, that young man is taken to you. After all this time to spot you in a crowd and stop to say hello. I can't imagine, my daughter, out with the Prince."

Giggles and laughter break out around Maria's naiveness. Morena continues teasing her friend, "After you're married, I'm moving to the castle with you. I will be your handmaiden," she laughs.

Alazaar, watching in the crowd, is heartbroken. He knows he has nothing to offer compared to the Prince, and that he will never have Maria's heart. Try as he has, she just doesn't have the feelings for him he has for her.

Time goes on, and Prince Phillip and Maria's courtship becomes serious as feelings for each other blossom. One evening while having dinner in the castle, the Prince gains everyone's attention.

"Please, everyone, may I speak?" he asks. The room quiets down.

"Family, friends, guests, a few months ago we had a dance. And at that dance I had the pleasure and joy of meeting this lovely girl of our Kingdom. Since then, this amazing lady has stolen my heart. Her beauty, her smile, her character is like nothing I've seen of anyone else in our Kingdom. She is intelligent and wise, and even occasionally chastises me." Laughter breaks out in the room. "Of course, I am speaking of this very lovely lady, Maria Alexander."

The crowd breaks out in applause as the Prince goes down on one knee in front of her. Taking her hand, he asks, "Maria, you have my heart, and now I wish to give you my life. I love you. Would you do me the honor of marrying me?"

The crowd gasps in surprise. Maria covers her mouth with her hand. The King and Queen are shocked. The room goes silent as all eyes focus on Maria.

Maria begins to cry. She nods her head affirmatively as she reaches to hug the Prince. "Yes Phillip. I love you too. Yes, I will marry you."

The two fall into each other's arms, their lips join together, expressing their love in front of everyone.

Within a month they are married. It was an amazing, beautiful, fairytale wedding. The celebration was huge, as members from all over the Kingdom attended the event that lasted for days. Festivities went well into each night. Shops and markets all closed as the city embraced and welcomed Her Royal Highness Maria Alexander.

Alazaar died to self that day. His loss tearing a hole in his heart that could never be filled. And, with Alazaar's demise, Morena was also destroyed, knowing Alazaar would never feel the love for her that he did for Maria. Morena knew she couldn't fill the void in Alazaar's heart; and that her love for Alazaar would never be returned. Both were destined to feel the pain of rejection forever. After all the years of trying. All the support they had given. Both were not seen by the recipients of their love.

Both also decided that day, vengeance would come someday for the betrayal they have been handed.

Tragedy Strikes

Years pass....

Prince Phillip and Her Royal Highness Maria were happy. Times were good in the Kingdom, and in the castle. Morena did become Maria's handmaiden and moved into the castle as well. Prince Phillip and Alazaar even developed a friendship over time, and Alazaar remained loyal to the Prince. In time he too takes a position in the castle maintaining his friendship with Morena, Maria, and Phillip.

In time, Prince Phillip and Maria were blessed with a child, a boy. Everyone was excited that an heir to the throne had been born. They named him James. Prince James was adored by his parents and was given all the attention a child could want. He was taught to read, to write, to be respectful, to dance; everything that was required of a Prince was passed on.

When James was four years old, tragedy struck. King Germaine passed away. His grandfather was gone. And even at four years old, he felt the loss.

Prince Phillip was crowned King Phillip Edmonds of the land, his wife now Queen Maria Edmonds. Life went on.

James grew into a loveable precious young man who only knew happiness and kindness, until that fateful day. He was sixteen years old the day his mother was murdered.

It was a day like any other. Sunny, joyful, laughter...until the scream heard throughout the Kingdom.

James was enjoying lunch, chatting about recent activities and the latest hunting expedition with his friends when a scream shrieked through the castle. He jumped from his chair and ran upstairs. There is crying and wailing coming from his parents' quarters. He enters, finding two maids kneeling beside his mother, laying dead on the floor. His father sits on the bed, his head in his hands. Blood flows across the floor from his mother's body, a knife protruding from her neck.

"Mom!" James rushes to be beside his mother. Tears pour from his eyes as he buries his face into his mother's body. He looks up, "Father!" he cries.

Blood drips from his father's hand as he rests upon the bed. "Father, what happened? What did you do? Why?"

King Phillip begins to cry. "I...I do not know what happened. We were...." he stops to think.... "We were talking. We went to breakfast, we returned to our chambers, I felt tired and so I laid down, your mother beside me. I woke up at the sound of a scream, your mother was on the floor, a knife in her neck, my hand covered with blood."

He cries hard, "Maria, oh my Maria. What has happened?"

Morena enters the room and looks at the scene. She sheds not a single tear but attends to James to comfort him. She looks to King Phillip, "Your Majesty? What have you done?"

The King looks at his murdered wife. "Something evil has done this. I loved Maria. And I remember nothing. Someone has done this, caused this. But why? Who would do such a thing? Maria was a good person, and a good Queen to the people."

Morena offers, "We shall find out what has happened Your Majesty, and someone will pay."

She escorts James from the room. In the hallway outside is Alazaar. She greets him and smiles. "The Queen is dead," she remarks, and grins.

Alazaar's heart tears in two. Even though he never had Maria, his love for her never waned. Now however, King Phillip would know his pain, the loss of the beloved that was taken from him.

Over the next few days, Maria is buried, and the Kingdom mourns her loss. Several days later, Morena drags a young man before the King. "You were poisoned Your Majesty."

"What? Morena, what is the meaning of this? Who is this man?"

"This man drugged you Your Majesty - the day Queen Maria was killed. We found these drugs in his quarters. He is not from here Your Majesty. A spy, from who knows where."

145

The young man of twenty-two or twenty-three falls to his knees. "Your Majesty, I am being falsely accused, I have been working in the gardens. I know nothing of these drugs."

"Silence!" Shouts Morena. "Liar! Your Majesty, in addition to the drugs, we found this, a set of knives." She opens the case, containing five knives. "There is one missing. These knives match the knife used to kill our beloved Queen. This set was also found in a cupboard in his quarters. Our guess is the poison he used is being grown in our own gardens. He said it himself; 'he has been working the gardens.'"

The King looks around the room. "Is there anyone who can vouch for this man?"

The room remains silent as people look at each other. No one dares speak up by order of Morena.

The King looks to the man, "Why have you done this to us?" But the man only cries and says not a word.

"Very well. Because you have done this, justice is demanded. I sentence you to death by the guillotine. Take him away."

The man sobs and maintains his innocence as he is led away.

The next day, he is executed.

King Phillip is changed by the death of his beloved Maria. Happiness leaves the Castle, his dedication to James declines. He demands the Prince remain in the castle at all times to avoid danger. The kitchen staff are replaced out of fear of conspiracy against the throne.

He appoints Alazaar and Morena as his closest advisors, giving Morena the power she has always dreamed of.

Two years pass....

Prince James turns eighteen. Alazaar has always been loyal to his father, and a friend to himself, but he grows concerned that the power Alazaar now holds will be abused.

But, at this time he can only hope for what is best. He begins to travel the Kingdom, learning of what is happening. The Kingdom is being run by Alazaar, the King's court has been abolished, his father still steeped in deep depression, there is nothing for him back at the castle. While away, in a small village, he meets a young woman, Amira. Amira's community is a farming community nestled in the western hills of the Kingdom. Goats and sheep run among the hills, and Prince James find some peace there. He decides to stay in the village for a long period. In time, Amira captures his heart, and they have a simple wedding attended by only Amira's friends and family. The young Prince is happy and in love.

After a year, he returns to the castle with his bride. His father is delighted to hold his son in his arms again. Morena and Alazaar are not as welcoming, but James is happy with his wife, and they leave the affairs of the Kingdom to Alazaar.

Nine months later, a little girl is born. They name her Destiny.

Dark Times

"Morena! Where is Morena?" The King screams, wanting his closest advisor to once again calm his fears regarding the state of the Kingdom.

"Morena!"

"Yes, Your Majesty, I'm here," she responds as she walks into the throne room.

"Morena, I am concerned the people no longer respect me. The Kingdom is falling apart. I fear for the life of James. I miss my beloved Maria still to this day so much."

"Try and be at peace my King. The Kingdom is loyal to you, Alazaar and I are loyal to you. May I suggest you give Alazaar power as Governor over the people to deal with the insurrectionists, and trade problems that have arisen? Then you can be more at peace and continue your focus to find James."

King Phillip rests his head on his hand as he sits in his chair upon the throne. He is weak, and tired. His energy drained from the self-imposed lack of the purpose since Maria's death.

"Perhaps you are right Morena. I have no will to guide the Kingdom anymore. Perhaps it is time to appoint someone I trust."

Morena smiles at the King's words, seeing her power increase even more. Her evil curses spoken daily over Alazaar and the King. As her evil grows, so too her power grows.

The next day, a notice is sent out to all the Kingdom.

"By order of the King. Let it be known that from this day forward, Alazaar Demitri Holden is appointed as Governor over all the lands of the Kingdom of Cradora. It is further decreed that all loyal subjects will abide by the rule of law established under his Governorship. The penalty for failure to abide by these laws will be severe. So sayeth the King."

"Signed King Phillip Edmonds."

Morena approaches Alazaar. "I have convinced the King to appoint you as Governor over all the Kingdom. I promise you he will pay for what he did to your beloved Maria. First he steals her from you all those years ago, then he murders her, and he gets away with it. I will avenge us both."

Morena has been planning her revenge for years for what happened that broke both her heart, and Alazaar's. She is more evil now than good, her craft of black magic and curses taking over her soul.

Alazaar smiles, believing now she to be an ally, "Morena. You have always supported me and cared for me, and I've always cast you aside. Please forgive me. I see now your devotion to me, and I cherish you as my friend."

Alazaar goes and kneels before the King. "My King, I am honored that you have chosen me to govern the people. We will maintain law and order, while allowing the people to prosper. I will make sure your name is revered in all the lands Your Majesty."

"Thank you Alazaar, I knew I could trust you. The people deserve a good life, and we must make sure the opportunities exist for them to thrive."

"Yes Your Majesty. I will see that it happens."

He stands and leaves the throne room. Plans develop in his head. He does not wish to kill the King, but to ruin him, leaving him in disgrace, holding him responsible for his loss of Maria.

Meanwhile Morena uses curses that plague the King with paranoia and hauntings of Maria. The nightmares of Maria extracting the knife from her neck and handing it back to Phillip causes many sleepless nights. In his paranoia state, he believes he is losing control of the Kingdom, thus supports Alazaar's rules.

King Phillip still has no recollection of what happened in those moments of that fateful day. He feels sometimes as though he is losing his mind. The only thing that keeps him going is his love for James.

Alazaar begins work setting up a local structure of troops, an army, which can be used against the people. An army of his own. Those not willing to support his rules are executed quickly. Fear spreads through the Kingdom as Alazaar and Morena begin their reign of terror.

High taxes are levied against the people. Each month, payments for all types of services are pressed upon them all. Taxes on purchases, taxes to travel, taxes on animal feed, taxes on farm seed, taxes on their property. The people begin to suffer at the hands of the corrupt policies.

New laws go out, curfews are set, people become more restricted. Villages are raided, women and men taken prisoner. Marauders and vigilantes are hired to collect the taxes and enforce the laws.

People begin to revolt. Rebels and insurrectionists arise. Violence breaks out in the villages and in Artems.

Alazaar inquires about the Kingdom's natural resources and how they are used. He learns the most valuable is the minerals from the small mining operation done at Two Springs.

He quickly seizes the operation.

Taxes fall delinquent, people become poorer. Markets close, and hard times fall upon everyone.

Meanwhile the King is oblivious, drowning in his sorrow and depression. His only informants now Morena and Alazaar. He hears what they want him to hear.

James, Amira, and Destiny do well and stay in the background. But soon he hears rumors of the hard times in the Kingdom. He travels back to the castle to see for himself what is happening. He wonders why his father would allow this.

Upon investigation, he sees firsthand the plight of the people. He returns to his father only to be intercepted by Morena.

"James. your father has missed you, how are you today? What have you been hiding?"

"Not hiding Morena, I have heard rumors and have seen for myself what is happening. The people and the Kingdom are not well. What has my father done? I must speak with him."

"James, your father is aware of everything and in complete control. Do not take to heart what lazy and poor people complain about. There will always be those who are dissatisfied."

"No Morena. It's not like that." James heads to speak with his father.

"James my boy, you have returned to us. where have you been? I have missed you for so long. Come and sit, let us talk."

"Hello father. Yes, we must talk. Father, I have heard horrible rumors that the Kingdom is not well. People are going hungry. Animals are dying because of lack of food. Our neighbors no longer wish to trade with us. What has happened father?"

"Nonsense James. Alazaar and Morena have complete control over everything. The Kingdom is doing wonderful. The treasury is full, the people are happy."

"No father, you are wrong. I have ridden through Artems. I have been to several villages. I was spat at, and stones were thrown at me. The Kingdom is not well."

"James, I shall talk with Alazaar and get to the bottom if this. There is nothing to worry about. Now go, return to your wife and daughter. Please, I will handle it."

For the first time in many years, James sees that his father is not well. He thought he had been suffering from a mental sickness due to blaming himself for the death of his mother. We explained that was not his fault having been under the influence of poison. But now, now James realizes that his father is not aware of what is happening. He is out of touch with the Kingdom.

Morena, listening from the hall, now sees James as a threat. She scurries away quickly to keep from being seen.

Morena goes to Alazaar, "Alazaar, James has arrived. I thought your men had been watching for him. No matter. He's been outside the city, and some villages. He knows what is happening."

"Do not fret my dear Morena. Soon I will finalize the army and take complete control. Then we will become royalty my dear."

Later that day the King calls to speak with Alazaar.

"Alazaar. James has informed me that not all is well in the city, nor in the Kingdom. I have trusted you to oversee things, but perhaps now it is time for me to involve myself once again. I'm sure you've done a fine job, but I wish to speak with the King's court. Can you have them assembled tomorrow please?"

"Yes Your Majesty, I will see too it."

"Thank you Alazaar. You have been a good friend."

The Executioner Arises

Alazaar calls for his Generals and speaks to Morena. "The time has come. Now is the time to take what is ours. The King wishes to speak with the court tomorrow. It is then that we will take control. Let us summons the King's court for a meeting tomorrow after noon."

Morena smiles with glee at hearing Alazaar's words. "All these years of waiting, of planning; vengeance will be ours."

Word is sent out to the members of the King's court, who have not convened since Alazaar was made Governor, a meeting will be held the next afternoon.

The next afternoon everyone is assembled in the courtroom. There are murmurs and concerns expressed as everyone has been kept in the dark for so long. Many are angry that the King has allowed things to get so distraught and demand answers.

As everyone takes a seat, the doors open for the King, along with James, to make their entry. A few minutes later the King and Prince enter the room. All rise and clap, delighted to see both of them in good health and appearing before them.

King Phillip takes his seat. Prince James sits to his right, Alazaar to his left. "Greetings my friends," he says, opening the session. "As you're all aware, it has been a long time since I have been involved with our beloved Kingdom. I can only offer that after the death of our beloved Queen, I spiraled into a deep depression that I was unable to break free of. However, do not fret, for thanks to our dear Prince James, I am returning to my senses."

Applause breaks out as everyone welcomes back the King.

"Now then, the first order of business. James is concerned that things are not as well in the Kingdom as I've been led to believe. I would like to hear from each of you as to the conditions of your regions."

Alazaar stands up. "Your Majesty, I wish to welcome the elite members of your court."

King Phillip interrupts him. "Thank you Alazaar, but that is not necessary at this time. You and I speak every day, and they know you well. I wish very much to hear from our members. Some have travelled far to be with us today."

"I understand Your Majesty, but I must insist, if you will grant me just one moment, we can clear up a lot of misunderstanding." With that he points to the rear guards.

At the signal the guards open the doors. Morena enters the room, followed by armed soldiers with swords, and bows with arrows drawn.

"Alazaar, what is the meaning of this? How dare you draw weapons against my court!" screams King Edmonds.

Alazaar steps behind the King and removes his crown. Placing it on his own head, he remarks. "As of today, Your Majesty, consider yourself de-throned. I am now your King, and you will kneel before me."

He pulls the King out of his chair and holds a sword to his throat. "Kneel. Or both you and your son die now."

King Phillip kneels and asks for mercy on his son. Two members of the court jump to defend the King and are immediately cut down by arrows.

"Stop!" yells James. "Why Alazaar? Why are you doing this? Morena, explain your actions."

"We are collecting on a very old debt James. One that was made years before your birth. Made at a time when your beloved father was just a young Prince. Your father destroyed our lives you see. Without concern for commoners, he stole your mother from us. Now he pays for his actions."

"But my father loved my mother. And you all were the best of friends.

Morena, my mother brought you to the Castle as her handmaiden. She always treated you with kindness and love."

"Your mother broke my heart and ruined my life. Her handmaiden. I despised being in her employ. The best day of my life was when I had her killed at the hands of your own father," she laughs hysterically.

"What are you saying? You killed my mother? The poison? The gardener?"

"Oh yes, him. Poor young man was in the perfect place to take the fall. A bit of poison, and the curse I put upon your father, and he slit your mother's throat with ease. Weak-minded old fool."

"Morena, you did this? I have trusted you as a confidant all these years, and now you tell me you are responsible for the death of Maria?" asks the King.

Morena walks over beside the King. "Oh, I do suppose I mourned Maria's death for a few moments, but seeing you wither and weep at the sight of her dead body.....I got over it fast." She laughs and walks to Alazaar.

She raises her arm, pointing to Alazaar, "Alazaar is now King. And you," she sweeps her hand across the room, "you are all condemned to death. We shall rule the kingdom now as we wish."

Alazaar kicks the King over to the ground and laughs. The soldiers open fire on the members of the court. Arrows fly and bodies fall. In the end, only Phillip and James remain.

"Take this man to the dungeon," says Alazaar, pointing to King Phillip. "And send guards to the Market. Kill everyone who is there. It has come to my attention that the wife and daughter or our beloved Prince are shopping today."

"And you! Young James, you may live, but only to do as I command in front of the people. If you do not, your father meets the same fate as your wife and daughter do this day."

The King and James are taken to the dungeon. Tears run down James' face as he thinks about his wife and young daughter. He prays that they are far from the market by this time.

Soldiers storm the marketplace, and it is a slaughter. Bodies are everywhere. Amera and Destiny fall in the battle.

Back at the castle, Alazaar sits upon the throne. "Morena, my dear, come."

Morena goes and stands by Alazaar.

"Morena, now that I am King, I am in need of a Queen. You have always been my best ally, a true friend. Will you now become my Queen?"

Morena smiles, "Why Alazaar, I thought you'd never ask. Yes my dear, it will be my honor to become your Queen."

Morena finally gets the love from Alazaar she has always dreamed of.

Two days later, James is led out of the castle to a meager house. "This is your new residence now. We suggest you do as Alazaar commands. The bodies of your beloved wife and daughter have been brought to the courtyard for you to bury," says the Guard.

James runs to the courtyard and drops. He wails loudly, in tears. He pulls the two bodies into his arms. Friends have been made aware and come to his aid. Amera and Destiny are buried, and James retracts from society.

Chapter EIGHT: A New Queen

Tyranny Setback

The warmth of the morning sun upon my face feels wonderful. The sand beneath my body is actually comfortable; molded to my shape after laying there all night. My arm is around Gemma, her head resting on my chest. The sound of birds and the water rippling over rocks is pleasant.

I wake up the next morning enjoying the serenity, but those thoughts are quickly replaced with thoughts of my father's beheading the day before.

Then I hear Gemma say, "Good morning Your Majesty," as she leans over and kisses me on the lips.

I caress her face, "Good morning my future Queen."

"Did you sleep at all?" she asks.

"Yes, some. It still seems surreal."

She pats me on the chest. "I'm here for you, we all are, as I've said. No one should have to watch their father die in that manner."

I nod and sit up. "Yes, my father is gone, but he was a good man and taught me well about the affairs of the Kingdom. He just put his trust in the wrong man. But I am now betrothed to the most amazing lady I've ever known. I'm sure my father would approve of you sitting in my mother's seat beside me someday on the throne."

"Well, I certainly don't feel worthy of such a place, but I will always cherish being by your side."

We get up and head for coffee. The men have a plan to get the rail from the mine and have already started acting on it.

"Good morning Your Majesty," they say as I walk in for coffee.

Orien greets me. "There are still no words for what we witnessed yesterday Your Majesty, we all offer you once again our heartfelt condolences."

"Thank you. I thank all of you for everything you have done for our Kingdom. I pledge not to fail you as your new King."

Katherine brings over the morning coffee as others scurry about their morning getting ready for today's activities.

"Gemma, in light of yesterday's events, I think we should postpone our trip to Westerly for a couple weeks. I'm sorry, but I fear Alazaar is not finished with his rampage. I promise you; we will go my love."

She rubs my back, "I completely understand James, and I totally agree. We should wait and see what happens next."

"Thank you my dear."

The morning goes slow. Everyone is still in shock as to what happened yesterday, and thus concerned about the state of the Kingdom and what Alazaar will do next.

That afternoon a rider comes from Artems with news. "Your Majesty, I have news from Alazaar. He has announced that the rebels will be hunted down and executed, and until that happens, five people will be randomly selected and executed every week. … starting next Saturday."

The room goes silent at the news. "Well, that gives us a week to form a new plan. Another rescue," I say.

Gemma asks, "James, that will be even more dangerous, but you're right. We can't let him just slaughter people."

"Agreed. No doubt he is delighted at the thought of using that

158

guillotine again. We must destroy it. Orien, do we have any of those explosives left?"

"Yes Your Majesty. More than enough to take care of that."

I turn to the rider, "did Alazaar give a time?"

"Yes, Your Majesty. 2:00 in the afternoon, just like yesterday. If I may Your Majesty, please accept my deepest sorrows on behalf of your father. He was a good man, and a good King. We all loved him and felt his care for each of us. The loss of the Queen would have devastated the strongest of men."

"Thank you young man, I appreciate that. What is your name?" I ask.

"My name is Lucas. Your friend Mark sent me. He wishes you well."

"Thank you Lucas, when you've rested your horse and eaten, please return to Mark and tell him I will be in touch."

"Yes, Your Majesty, as you wish."

"Katherine, please bring Lucas some food. Thank you."

Katherine waves and nods and serves Lucas.

Gemma asks, "Destroy the guillotine? It's huge. Do you have an idea how?"

"I do, but it's risky. I want to destroy his machine in front of everyone. I want him to witness its destruction."

Orien speaks up, "I love that idea Your Majesty."

"I know every inch of that castle, and every secret door. We can get in, set the explosives, and get out way before charges are detonated. We're going to need a lot of wire though, and be able to disguise it, so its hidden as the guillotine rolls out from storage."

Ryan speaks up. "We can get wire from Timbervale, and a thin wire can be buried in the dirt. We can rig something under the bottom of the guillotine to lay and cover the wire. The guards pushing it will never notice."

"That's perfect Ryan, thank you."

"Maybe we could rig up some of those fireworks Mark left, so as to turn it's destruction into a celebration at the same time?" Gemma remarks.

The room fills with laughter at her idea.

"We can make that happen too. That's a super idea Gemma," says Orien.

"Alazaar will be so pissed. Splendid idea my dear. Oh, I would love to see his face as he witnesses that." I reply.

"On another subject, Gemma we need to send a rider to Westerly to announce our plans to visit in the coming weeks. Any ideas who to send?"

Before Gemma can answer, Camilla speaks up. "Nadia and I will go Your Majesty. We know the way."

"Wonderful, I shall write a letter and seal it for delivery. I do not have my father's seal, so explain to them I only have my ring, and it's been sealed with it." Since Camilla and Nadia did such a wonderful job rescuing the women, I feel certain they will be safe traveling to Westerly.

"Oh James, my dear, we can have the blacksmith surely forge you a seal of your own." Gemma remarks. "I'll handle that for you."

"Even more wonderful. Thank you my dear."

Gemma excuses herself and heads to the blacksmith shop. I make my way to the cavern to see the latest.

By Friday a plan is developed to destroy the guillotine in front of everyone. Word has been sent ahead to Mark, who waits for us.

We travel to Artems and connect with Mark. Alazaar's soldiers are everywhere, and tensions are high. Under the cover of darkness, we approach the castle. As a boy I used to play in the various tunnels, moving through trap doors, fake walls, and inner walls. Getting close to the guillotine is not an issue. The concern is how many guards will there be?

The night is very chilly and the moon casts very little light, both of which play in our favor. I lead Gemma, Orien, Mark, and Ryan through the castle maze and arrive at the gate nearest the guillotine.

Orien remarks, "I count six guards."

Gemma adds, "There's two more over there."

The good news is all the guards are huddled around fires to stay warm. Not only does this distract them, but it also makes the shadows even more hidden. Ryan and Mark make their way quickly across the short distance to the machine and slide underneath it out of sight. The rest of us stand ready for a fight, and to escape should the need arise.

Ryan, with Mark's help, sets the explosives and the wire to the belly of the guillotine. A blade leans down, cutting into the dirt only about an inch. As the guillotine is pushed forward, the wheels will turn the wire wheel releasing the wire. It runs down the blade and into the dirt. The plow shape of the blade slightly covers the wire, burying it so as not to be seen. That's the plan anyway.

When the machine is in place the next day, all the wheels will be locked to keep it from rolling. Orien designed a switch that connects the wires to the explosives, to the wires laid underground. This tightens the wire.

At the back of the overhang where the guillotine is stored, we rig a charge to ignite a fuse, using thin cloth filled with black powder. The last piece is the connection to the blade lever. When the blade is raised and locked in place, the fuse will be pulled rapidly along the buried wire, thus connecting the charge to the explosives.

When the locks are in place, a lever releases the igniter. The fuse lights, burns rapidly, and boom. Orien and Ryan are geniuses.

Ryan and Mark make haste of the work and return to us. Everything is set. We make our way out of the castle and back to Mark's. He has set up a room for Gemma and me, Orien and Ryan get comfortable in the bunkhouse.

Gemma comes over and puts her arms around my neck, "We did it. Now if it only works. Five people are depending on us."

"I hear your concern, but it will work. I have complete faith in Orien and Ryan. Their skills are amazing." I kiss her while pulling her tightly to me. Her lips are moist and warm, and the scent of her hair is captivating. "I love you, Gemma."

"I love you too.... my King." She giggles while having fun with my title. "And I know the guys are amazing, and I'm sure it will work as well. I just can't help but think about the men Alazaar plans to execute."

"I know. I think of them too, but not only will we save them tomorrow, we will destroy that infernal machine. Alazaar will not easily replace it quickly, buying us some time hopefully."

"I hope he's standing on it when it blows," she says.

"That would be a huge win if so, but I doubt he will be. I suspect setup of the machine will happen prior to his arrival, but it will be good enough."

Gemma and I lay down next to each other, kiss each other, and try to get some sleep.

"Goodnight Gemma."

"Goodnight James."

The next day we hang around the tavern with Mark and his friends. Mark is a good man and a good friend. It's colder today than yesterday, but Gemma planned well and brought warm clothes for us, and it is not our plan to hang around after the event. Once the fireworks are over, God willing, we will quickly return to the cave.

The afternoon rolls around slowly, as our anxiety increases at a phenomenal pace. We can only hope and pray. The guards usually roll the machine to the courtyard about fifteen minutes prior to execution time, We make our way to our same viewing area as before, knowing we will be out of danger there.

The time arrives and we make our way to the roof top. The guillotine machine, while having its own fixed wheels, still rides along a greased track, in and out of storage. There is no turning or twisting, allowing for it to be moved easily by only a few men. And leaves us free from worry regarding the wire and fuse affixed to the underside.

As expected, at fifteen till two, men appear who begin pushing the guillotine to its spot in the courtyard. The courtyard here is just covered in grass for fun gatherings, and now executions apparently. My father would die a second time seeing this barbaric event.

The men follow standard procedures setting the machine in place. We are too far away to know if the wire wheel actually remained in place correctly, and the wire unwound as desired. We'll know in a few moments.

The guillotine is moved with ease. When it arrives at its spot, the men locked the wheels. Alazaar appears on the castle balcony. Soldiers march out and surround the machine. Morena joins him shortly thereafter.

The two men make their way up the stairs to the platform. They double check all the bracing that holds the blade mast in place.

Gemma squeezes my hand.

The men begin to raise the blade. With each pull of the rope the blade only raises a few inches. By design, the blade has mechanisms to keep it from falling accidentally. The irony.

Just a few more pulls. The blade hits the top, the men tie the rope and pull the brake.

The explosion sends the men flying. The guillotine shatters as pieces shoot high in the air. After the explosion, fireworks ignite. Huge balls of color explode overhead. Red, green, and yellow sparks fill the sky. The crowd erupts in enormous applause and cheers. The remains of the guillotine burn brightly as guards and soldiers run back inside the castle.

Alazaar and Morena just stand on the balcony, watching as there next round of wickedness evaporates in the smoke. Alazaar turns and walks back inside.

The five of us light up with joy but know that danger is still everywhere. The explosion was loud enough to be heard throughout the city. Bells are ringing, people are cheering. We make our way back to our horses and head home.

We arrive back at the cave and word of our success spreads fast. Gemma leaps from her horse and runs to embrace me. Our lips melt together as she falls into my arms.

"We did it. We did it, again," she exclaims.

"Long live King Edmonds. Long live the King," the crowd shouts. I wave my hand, and we walk inside. Katherine and Madelene are both there to greet us. Hugs and handshakes are everywhere.

Meanwhile, back at the castle, Alazaar sits on his throne. Morena stands beside him. Loyal supporters stand around somberly in silence. The two senior generals enter the room.

"King Alazaar, we have imprisoned the guards watching over the guillotine last night. We have uncovered a wire that was used in some manner. We are still piecing this all together, but we will find those responsible for this, Your Majesty."

Alazaar stands and walks down to them. "Kneel before your King."

The two men kneel.

"Let me see your sword." He says to the one closest. The general hands over his sword.

"My two top generals. My most trained soldiers. This is a fine sword. In the right hands, an exceptional weapon. In the wrong hands a complete waste of exceptional craftsmanship."

Alazaar in a split-second swings the sword, and the heads of both men fall to the floor.

"Now, to those witnessing; this is how it is used in the right hands." He returns to his chair. "Find me two men worthy of this sword."

Several members leave the room.

Time Away

The next morning at the Cave, everyone is of good cheer. The overwhelming success of yesterday's event is going to be celebrated for a long time.

At morning coffee I compliment Ryan, "You're engineering feats just continue to amaze me Ryan. Between Orien and yourself, I know we will be successful in our endeavors to regain our Kingdom."

"Thank you Your Majesty. But it's again your leadership that encourages us all to continue."

I chuckle, knowing he is being kind.

Gemma and her mom come in from outside and approach us enjoying our coffee. Gemma is bursting, I can tell she is planning something.

"Good morning my dear James. How is our King feeling this wonderful morning?" she asks smiling, excited and glancing at her mom.

"I'm well my love. You are certainly joyous. What is going on?"

Gemma takes a deep breath. "James, I've thought about it and thought about. I love you, and each of these crusades we take are dangerous. I don't know the future, but I know I want to be your wife more than anything, and if we are to die soon through some horrible twist of fate, I want to die as your wife."

She sits on my lap and puts her arm around me.

"You know I feel the same way Gemma. What are you thinking?"

"My dear James, Your Majesty, I don't need or want a fancy wedding in a far-off castle surrounded by people I don't know. I want to get married here, surrounded by friends and family we love. And I don't want to wait until we take back the Kingdom and lose all that time, testing fate that something happens to one of us. So, forgive me if this is inappropriate, but can we get married here? ....Today?"

She blushes pure red, knowing that is very uncustomary to suggest such a thing, The room falls silent waiting on my reaction, my response.

With her on my lap, I stand, her now in my arms. My heart leaps as her words sink into my mind. I twirl and dance, looking at nothing but her eyes. She laughs and holds me tight as I move across the floor. Our lips meet once more as I lower her to her feet.

"Yes, Gemma. I will happily marry you here, today. I love you with all that I am and want you by my side each moment forward. I firmly believe that together will be strong enough to withstand anything Alazaar can throw at us."

"I need a best man. Orien, I would be honored if you will stand with me."

"It will be my honor Your Majesty." He bows gracefully.

Gemma exudes happiness, "Mom, Dad, we have a wedding to finish planning."

Madelene and Erik raise their arms in applause, leading to loud cheers from all. Gemma selects Abbie as her Maid of Honor.

"I have to ask the obvious. As King I cannot marry myself. Is there a man of God in the community?"

"YES," exclaims Gemma, Robert is a friar. He just doesn't dress as one. ROBERT!" she yells, "has anyone seen Robert?"

A few minutes later Robert appears and is told of our needs.

"It would be my honor to marry you Gemma. I have watched you grow from a playful child to the beautiful young woman I see before me today. The King could not have chosen a more perfect girl."

Gemma gives Robert a huge hug, then dashes to her mom's side to get ready. They flurry off to do wedding stuff.

"Well, that was not expected. I wonder, should I finish my cup of coffee?" I say rhetorically as everyone laughs.

Katherine is right there, "Don't you dare Your Majesty. I will bring you a fresh cup."

Orien and I shake hands, and he pats my upper arm. Erik comes over and echoes his congratulations as well once more.

"Your Majesty. How honored am I that you and my dear Gemma are to be married. She's a handful at times, but she has a good heart, and the people of the Kingdom will love her. Her mother and I truly wish you both the most happiness."

"Erik, you are about to be my father-in-law, please call me James."

"No sir Your Majesty. That would not be appropriate. Before being my son-in-law, you are my King. It must be that way."

"Very well Erik. I am still young in many ways. Thank You. Now where did that daughter of yours go?"

Orien grabs my arm, "Oh no sir, it's bad luck to see the bride on her wedding day. Even if she did just suggest that today is your wedding day. You come with us and let the women have their time."

We all laugh and head to the cavern. There's always work to be done.

"Hey Orien, so where abouts did you come by the explosives that were used yesterday?"

"There is a supplier in a neighboring village. I'm not sure, but I think he creates it himself. I can take you there someday if you like."

"Yes, I would like that very much. Do you think he is loyal to us?"

"Absolutely Your Majesty. He was very loyal to your father, and I know he will be loyal to you as well. He's a good man."

"But the fireworks came from the Orient through eastern suppliers. I'm not sure how Mark acquires those. That is a whole different craft."

"I understand. Fireworks will not be necessary. Thanks."

Arriving at the cavern area, I can see the west entrance has been cut through. The added sunlight enhances the natural beauty of the cavern. It is easy to see where buildings and homes are being laid out. It all looks amazing.

By midafternoon, Orien and several of the men beckon me to come with them to the river. I follow. Once there Orien exclaims, "Now."

With that, four men pick me up and throw me in the river, fully clothed. I am caught completely off-guard. I rise out of the water, it's barely waist deep, hearing the laughter and jeers of the men.

Orien yells, "You're getting married Your Majesty. Time for a bath." One of the men tosses me a bar of soap. "And since the guillotine has been destroyed, we know we are safe from your wrath for doing this. Your bride is expecting a clean man." They are all laughing hysterically at my demise.

"No wrath here my good friends. I love you all. And yes, Gemma will be pleased. But you could have just made the suggestion." I shout back laughing as I remove my clothing and begin to wash myself.

"Sorry Your Majesty. This is a ritual of betrothed men in our community dating back generations, the groom is thrown into a pool of water for bathing on his wedding day. We don't have a pool, so you get the river. Either way, you are one of us sire," shouts Warren.

"I am both humbled and proud. But now my clothes are all wet. Am I to wed naked?"

"Not at all. Gemma has been planning and hoping for this day for a long time. Here are clean and dry clothes for you, and a towel. Take your time and we will give you some privacy."

I simply wave my arm in thanks and goodbye for now. I've never felt more part of any community ever. I am honored they thought enough of me to throw me in the river. I laugh to myself and bathe. The water is cold, but I get used to it fast and enjoy a few moments of relaxation. Once finished I dry off, get dressed in my new clothes and return to the area outside the cave, where arrangements have been made for the wedding.

A short while later, everyone gathers and face away from the cave entrance, waiting for Gemma to make her appearance. I move to the front of them, along with Robert and Orien, and we wait.

Soon instruments begin to play. Erik waits at the rear of the crowd for his daughter to appear. Minutes later, Abbie walks out and to the front, then Gemma walks out. She is beyond beautiful. She's wearing the ankle length yellow dress in which I first saw her so many months ago. Her long brown hair, draping down over her shoulders. She has a wreath of green leaves and yellow flowers on her head. She looks up and her eyes meet mine as she takes her father's arm. Erik begins to walk her to the front of the crowd. Madelene is smiling and crying both.

Gemma and Erik arrive at the front and Erik hands me Gemma's hand. He kisses her on the cheek and returns to Madeline's side.

Gemma looks at me and blushes.

"You are stunningly beautiful, my dear Gemma."

"Thank you. We had nothing from which to make a white wedding dress. Do you find me acceptable in this?"

"My dear, it is absolutely stunning. It is because of that dress that I even saw you. It's perfect." I kiss her hand, and we face Robert.

Robert welcomes everyone and begins the ceremony. After some speaking, Gemma and I turn to face each other. Orien taps me on the shoulder. Abbie does the same for Gemma. We both look to our friends, and they hand us wedding rings, made in secret as a gift to us.

Robert says as tears form in Gemma's eyes, "These rings have been forged by the craftsmanship and love of this community. Please accept them as our gift to you. Forged in a circle, with no beginning and no ending. As you offer these rings to each other, know too that your love for each other now has no beginning and no end. Forever joined will you be.

I take Gemma's left hand and slide her ring onto her finger. She then does the same for me. "We this ring, I thee wed," we say in unison.

"King James, you may now recite your vows to Gemma," says Robert.

I take Gemma's hands in my mine, looking deep into her brown eyes, I recite, "Gemma, from the moment I saw you, you captured my heart. Since then, you have shown me the truest meaning of love. From this day forward, I pledge to you my life, my body, and my mind. I shall never forsake you, until death do we part."

"Your Royal Highness Gemma, you may now recite your vows to James."

Still holding hands, Gemma smiles and says, "James. I was not expecting at all what fate delivered to me that day we met. Since then, you have been beside me every step of the way. Because of you, I have come to know true love. From this day forward, I pledge to you my life, my body, and my mind. I shall never forsake you, until death do we part."

After a few more prayers and blessings, Robert announces....

"Ladies and Gentlemen, I present to you King James Edmonds and Queen Gemma Edmonds as husband and wife. You may kiss your bride Your Majesty."

Gemma laughs a happy laugh and our lips join together. The crowd goes crazy with applause and cheers. I walk Gemma a short distance back to her parents. They hug us both and congratulate us. We walk into the cave where once again, a banquet has been prepared. Hugs and tears are everywhere as well, once more.

Gemma and I sit side by side holding hands every chance we can as we are served magnificent plates of food. We are joined at the head table with Madelene, Erik, Orien, Abbie, Warren, Ryan, and Katherine. Music breaks out, and dancing commences. The celebration lasts well into the night.

As the party comes to a close I ask Gemma if she's ready for some sleep. She's been yawning more and more. Erik, Warren, and Katherine, come forward. "Your Majesty, Queen Gemma, several of us fixed up a little surprise for you. We'd like to show you something." Gemma and I look at each other, "You guys are the best. Lead the way."

We all walk to the cavern and towards the construction site. We come to a stop in front of a small cabin. Orien hands me a key. Katherine chuckles and leads Gemma to the door. "It's not much, but it's your Wedding day." I hand the key to Gemma. She turns and unlocks the door. Her face clearly shows her shock as she enters the room. Tears form in her eyes.

"Look at this James. This is amazing," she says.

The little cabin has been completed. It has a vanity station, a fireplace, side tables, and a luxurious bed, covered with pillows and quilts. The room is lit by candles in addition to the fireplace. Flowers adorn the place everywhere.

"This is truly special everyone. We thank you for all your effort and kindness," says Gemma.

Katherine announces, "okay, everybody out, we need to allow the newlyweds their privacy." A few last hugs and handshakes and Gemma and I find ourselves alone.

We hug and embrace each other and melt into a passionate kiss. We stop for air and just hold each other. "Let me freshen up," Gemma says. "Will you unzip my dress?"

There's no privacy in this cabin, but it doesn't bother Gemma, she lets her dress fall to the floor and walks to the vanity to wash up. I remove my shirt and my boots and sit on the edge of the bed.

"Did you hear the guys threw me in the river today?"

Gemma laughs, "Yes, I did. That is so wonderful. You really are a member of the community." She finishes cleaning up and turns to face me. She unbuttons her remaining clothing, unties the cord around her waist, and her under garments also fall to the ground. She stands there in front of me, completely naked. Her beauty in the fire-lit room is beyond description. She walks to me, as I stand up.

I can't take my eyes off her. She unbuttons my pants, and they fall to the floor. I pull her into my arms, our lips embrace again as I caress her soft, tender skin. We fall to the bed and consummate our marriage during a night of passion.

The next morning, I open my eyes and just admire Gemma laying next to me. The moment seems surreal. When Amira was murdered I thought I could never love again, and I still miss her. But I know she would want me to move on with life and would very much approve of Gemma.

Awhile later Gemma opens her eyes. Seeing me staring at her, she slides over next to me and snuggles. "Good morning my husband." She closes her eyes and rests her head on my chest.

"Good morning my Queen. Did you sleep?"

"mmmm, Like a baby," she says. "You?"

"Very well. But I could stay here all day with you, just like this."

She leans up on her arm and says, "With me? yes. Here? No." She runs her hands over my chest. "I have another surprise for you, my husband."

"You are so good to me." I caress her soft skin, enjoying the feeling of her next to me. I'm lost in ecstasy, far from the troubles of the Kingdom.

She jumps up, wide awake and thoroughly excited. "Come on, we have places to be."

"Do we? What are you up to now?"

She giggles, "You'll have to get up and see."

I roll my legs off the side of the bed, sitting up, enjoying the softness of the mattress, but loving the view as Gemma walks back to the wash bowl, naked.

She splashes cold water on her face and begins to get dressed. I follow her lead and do the same. The team that set this cabin up for us left clean clothes for both of us, some fruit, and jerky for breakfast.

We get dressed and ready to face the day. I open the door as Gemma pulls on her boots. I stand amazed at what I see. Gemma comes and puts her arms around me from behind. "Welcome to our honeymoon my love."

Outside is a horse-pulled coach, decorated to show off our newlywed status. It's as pretty a wedding coach as one would find anywhere. The bench is cushioned for comfort, and an open-air roof protects the occupants.

"That's amazing Gemma."

"Don't thank me. This is my from my mom, Abbie, Katherine, and many others that wish us well."

I kiss Gemma, "Where to first?"

"Are you serious? Coffee of course."

"I love you. Coffee it is." I help Gemma on the coach and off we go.

Through the new west entrance. No one is in sight out of respect for us on our wedding night. We ride around to the front of the cave and make our entrance.

Folks clap as we walk in. Katherine greets us first. "Good morning your Majesty and Queen Gemma. How was your sleep?"

"It was amazing. Thank you all for setting us up in such a nice way. I have never felt so much love," Gemma replies.

"Will you be having coffee with us?"

"Absolutely."

We take a seat. "So Gemma, where are we going?"

"James, arrangements have been made for us to get away a few days. You've been working hard, and we deserve a honeymoon. There is a private lake up north a few hours away. It is safe and quiet. It would just be us. Please James, may we go?"

"You are my Queen, my wife, my world. And you are wise beyond your years. Yes my Love. Time away with you sounds wonderful."

Gemma shrieks with happiness and begins kissing me. "It's all set. The coach is packed with everything we need thanks to our friends. It's going to be wonderful."

We finish some coffee and prepare to leave.

"Your Majesty, have a wonderful time. Enjoy time with Gemma. We'll take care of things around here a few days; the community and the Kingdom will be okay."

"Thanks Orien. I know everyone will be fine."

Erik and Madelene come to see us off as well. "Bye mom, bye dad. Don't worry, we'll be fine."

"Enjoy yourself dear."

175

I help Gemma climb onto the coach once more and we head out.

The Lake

The coach is comfortable, and Gemma sits very close, with her arm around my arm. I'm not too worried about safety given our direction and the recent event at the castle. Alazaar is surely trying to re-group his security, not knowing who to trust.

The trip is leisurely, and we chat about our future, the future of the community, and even the future of the Kingdom.

Gemma suggests, "James, a lot has happened, and I'm sure your mind is filled with worry and plans, but let's not think about nor talk about Alazaar and what has happened. Please? We just got married. A few days rest will be good for us."

"So right you are my dear. I only want to focus on you and start our life together with good memories. The Kingdom will be fine a couple of days."

The northern territory of the Kingdom is mountainous. Pine trees and rugged terrain as far as the eye can see. It's beautiful country, but not the easiest to inhabit.

After a few hours of riding, we arrive at our destination.

"Oh James, it's just how I remember it from my childhood."

We have arrived at a small mountain lake nestled in the forest. The water is crystal clear, and a waterfall feeds the lake continuously from the snow melt of higher elevations. A small sandy beach area is perfect for enjoying the sun while having a picnic. Behind the sandy area is a small cabin. It's not in the best of shape, but it's perfect. I guess the cabin to be over a hundred years old. Probably built by nomads long ago as a resting spot while transporting trade goods to the north.

We go inside, it's dusty and dirty. Clearly, no one has been here in a very long time. I walk over to Gemma and kiss her.

"It's amazing," I exclaim.

"Good, let's make it comfortable. I will light some candles and clean up. How about you start a fire darling."

I agree and head to the woods to collect firewood. Surely there is an abundance of it. Before long we have a warm fire blazing in the fireplace. Gemma has wiped down everything and the place is looking nice. She hands me a bucket she found in the corner.

"Would you please wash this out and bring me some water from the lake, please?"

"Of course my dear."

This time I walk to the lake side. I can see fish, so hoping that might be dinner the next few days. Lake trout are good eating. I wash the bucket out well and fill it for Gemma. The water is cold, but if we swim we can warm up by the fire after. In fact, that gives me the idea to start a fire outdoors for cooking and relaxing. But first I take the water to Gemma.

I unload the coach, finding a blanket to lay on the sand, then work on another fire. Gemma comes out a bit later. She walks to the water's edge and just admires the scenery.

"This is simply beautiful. Are you feeling good?" she asks.

"I feel fantastic, but I'll feel even better if you come and lay beside me."

We lay there a short time, relaxing in the sun. Although Gemma is not one to rest. She jumps up saying, "Come on, let's swim."

She strips naked and wades into the lake. When she gets waist deep she falls backward and floats.

She screams, "Brrrrr, that's cold! Come on James."

I stand up, strip and jump in. "Oh wow, cold is not the right word darling. How about frigid?"

Gemma laughs and swims to me. We embrace each other spinning around, dancing together, and playing in the water. Our bodies warm each other as we kiss and caress and fondle each other; exploring each other's bodies. She pushes away, splashing and kicking water at me. I chase her and she lets me catch her again. The world is far away as we just enjoy being young in the sun, sharing our love with each other.

After the cold takes over, we run to the blanket and sit by the fire. "James let's come here often," she says.

"Yes, I think as King, I should establish places like this throughout the Kingdom as sanctuaries of peace, so that many can enjoy the beauty of our Kingdom. But I may have to claim this spot just for us." I laugh.

We get dressed and try to catch some fish. Gemma has outdoor survival skills that way surpass mine.

She laughs, "James, my dear, you are never going to catch fish like that. Let me show you how to do it."

I am not too proud to let her teach me. She shows me the proper way to rig a pole from a branch, how to tie the knots, and what to find and use for bait. She explains what type of bugs trout like, and how to cast the line so that the bug just rests on top of the water. And sure enough, it doesn't take long before trout start leaping out of the water to catch the bugs.

"Nicely done! Now that you are catching them, do you know how to clean and cook them?" she asks.

"Actually, yes, I do. My father liked fish, so we would have fresh fish brought to the castle. I knew the kitchen staff very well and enjoyed learning about food preparation as part of my studies. Jasmine taught me to gut, prepare, and cook fish and other dishes."

"That's amazing. So, I've married both a King and a chef?" She laughs again, her hair slowly drying, her eyes sparkle with youth and beauty.

We prepare the meal and eat. Gemma brought additional fruits, vegetables, and seasonings providing us a well-rounded meal.

"Wow, this fish is wonderful James. You really can cook."

"Thanks, I enjoy it, but I seriously doubt once back at the castle I'll have much time for cooking."

"I've only been to the castle with you, seeing it from the roof tops. I can't wait to see the inside of it. I want you to show me every detail James."

"It will be my pleasure my dear."

We finish up dinner and go for a walk around the lake, holding hands and just having fun.

"It is so peaceful here." I remark.

We spend the evening relaxed. After dark, we return inside. The fire has it comfortably warm. I pull Gemma close, and our mouths melt together once more. Our tongues dance together as we intimately explore each other. I remove her clothes and begin kissing her body everywhere. We find our way to the bed and get lost in a night of passion and pleasure.

The next few days go by quickly with more of the same relaxing activities, swimming, eating, and passion, but we find the time has come to return to the community.

"These days have been wonderful James. I know it may be some time before we can enjoy anything like this again, but I shall never forget this. And as sad as I am about leaving, I'm also excited to see mom and dad, and our friends again."

"I agree, and I promise you we will be back here someday."

I hitch up the horses to the coach and we begin our journey home.

I have never felt so loved and so blessed.

Chapter NINE: A Warrior is Born

Allies Arrive

We arrive back home to hugs and kisses. Gemma's parents are super happy to have their daughter back. Orien and Warren give me a warm welcome as well; Katherine invites us to come and eat, it's what she does; and Gemma and I both laugh and oblige her. The trip home was several hours, and while wonderfully relaxing, we could eat.

We walk inside and to our great shock, there stands Princess Sarah and Alexandra.

"Well, this is an unexpected surprise." I hug Sarah and turn to Alexandra. She curtsies.

"Your Majesty, your runner arrived with your letter, but we soon received word of your father's execution. Our whole Kingdom mourns with you," she says.

"We are deeply sorry James. In light of all that, we believed it best for us to come here, and we brought one hundred soldiers with us as well. Of course, we had no idea you were away, but we arrived yesterday, and everyone has treated us well."

Gemma gets excited and hugs Alexandra, "It is so good to see you Alexandra."

"It's good to see you too. I hear you're ready to learn to fight. Although, I also hear you have already experienced a fight." Alexandra replies.

"Come, let's eat," says Madeline.

We meet still others. Everyone is happy to greet us, and all have questions about how our time away was.

"Our trip was peaceful, relaxing, and beautiful. The lake is just like I remember from years ago, Mom. Same cabin, now a clean cabin by the way, and great fishing. We swam, walked, and fried fresh fish. It was uncredible. But I'm also happy to be home," says Gemma.

"I'll second all of that. It was a wonderful time. We were both able to turn off all thoughts of past events, and just focused on being with each other. How's everything been here?"

Orien speaks up. "Well first off, we've tweaked the cabin you stayed in your wedding night. The King and Queen can't sleep on a cot like you were prior to your wedding. It's not the castle, but you two will be comfortable hopefully, and it's available everyday now for your use."

Gemma covers her gaping mouth, she's so excited to hear that. "You all are the best. We love each and every one of you. Isn't that fantastic James?"

"It is indeed. Thank you all so very much."

Princess Sarah says, "Wow, you all have done so much since we left the night of the women's rescue. And oh, how I would love to have seen Alazaar's face when that guillotine exploded. Very well done you all."

"We are blessed with many smart people. That's why I'm confident we will defeat Alazaar," I add.

"You certainly are," replies Sarah.

I ask, "Sarah, where are your men? Do they need anything?"

"They set up camp on the other side of the river, and no, they are well stocked. I didn't know what to expect upon our arrival, so we came prepared."

Ryan comes in, "Your Majesty, Queen Edmonds, we have unloaded the coach and tended to the horses. Your belongings have been returned to your cabin. If there is anything you need, please ask."

Gemma acknowledges the act of service, "Thank you Ryan. I have not seen Abbie since our return. Was she with you?"

"I'm here." Abbie comes walking in from the cavern side. "Yes, I was helping dad with your stuff. Welcome home, and how was your honeymoon?"

Gemma stands up and hugs Abbie. "You won't believe how amazing it was. I will tell you all about it later."

Madelene says, "You two have had a long day today. Why don't you take a walk? Your cabin is ready when you are. There's fresh linen and bedding, as well as fresh water. The guys also started a fire and restocked the firewood. It should be cozy for you."

"Thanks Mom, but I could have helped with all that."

"Gemma Edmonds! You will do no such thing. You are now Queen! There are people to take care of such things for you."

Gemma blushes, embarrassed for being called out about proper behavior in her new role. "Then what am I to do?" she asks.

"Learn to fight," says Alexandra. "Tomorrow morning, we start. We will integrate you with the soldiers just like the men."

"That will be wonderful. I am ready."

"We'll see about that this time tomorrow. Just because you're Queen now won't mean the men will go easy on you. We've instructed them that you are a trainee, just like any other. Sleep well tonight," says Sarah, playfully laughing.

"I am ready and will do as instructed Princess."

Orien adds, "And we hope to keep you busy tomorrow, Your Majesty, with plans to retrieve the rail from the mine. Now that you're back, if you approve, we need to act."

"You are absolutely correct my friend. The rail and the mine are so important. I'm curious, you told me once the mine supplies minerals and some gems. I never asked, what type of minerals?"

"Potassium nitrate mostly. They ship it to the ports for use on the boats in their cannons," says Orien.

"I knew you were going to say that. I just had a hunch, based on what I've seen, that potassium nitrate was being dug from there. So, we need sulfur and charcoal as well."

"We have the sulfur mines, James," says Sarah.

Abbie says, "Those are all common materials. What is special about those three."

Gemma asks, "I don't understand either. Why those three?"

I look at Orien, who knows exactly what I'm thinking. "Those minerals are the components for black powder, otherwise known as explosives. Black powder is used to fire ship cannons, used to fire muzzle loader rifles, and manufacture various other types of weapons. The factories on the ports mix them properly and make cannon balls and propellent packages. Potassium nitrate is the hardest to find in nature. So that's why Alazaar took over the mine so quickly. He knows the value of it."

"We may be out manned by Alazaar, but with enough explosives, we can have the advantage," I continue.

Gemma kisses me, "You're so smart."

Erik remarks, "Well I'll be damned, that is amazing. And we have access to plenty of charcoal as well."

Abbie again looks quizzical... "what is charcoal?"

Ryan responds, "Burnt wood embers my daughter."

"Oh, well we're not in short supply of that," replies Abbie.

"We can send you all the sulfur you want James," offers Sarah.

"Very well. We need to plan for gathering all these materials. That said, our first effort needs to be on the mine and the rail."

"I'm ready to help," says Gemma.

"Not so fast young lady, you aren't going anywhere except into training." Alexandra stops her cold. "We came all this way, mostly because of you. As Queen, being able to fight and understand violent conflict will make you a huge asset to your Kingdom."

"You're right Alexandra, and I'm ready."

"With that, my dear, let's take a walk. You are going to be very busy and very tired for several weeks," I say.

I take Gemma's hand, and we walk down by the river as usual.

"So, are you really ready to start training tomorrow?" I ask.

"I'm ready, but I'm also scared to be honest. I don't know what to expect, but I believe in Alexandra. She wants me up early to start. I asked if she would just knock on our door this first day and she agreed."

I kiss Gemma reassuring her she'll be fine, but training will be hard. Still, she's run and played in the woods her whole life and used to hard work. She'll be fine.

We sit in the sandy area. Tonight, though, we can hear the soldiers in the distance doing whatever soldiers do in the evening. Gemma takes my hand in hers.

"Hey. You're going to be fine." I tell her.

"I love you," she replies, and we get lost in kisses, sharing our lips and tongues - tasting and feeling intimate parts of each other. We head back to our cabin awhile later and pick up with the kissing. Only this time, naked.

The next day comes early with Alexandra knocking.

"Don't expect this type of royal treatment every day," Alexandra says chuckling.

Gemma comes and kisses me goodbye. "I will see you tonight my love. Wish me luck."

"It is the soldiers who will need luck my dear." I kiss her again and help her mount her house, then watch as they ride away. I am so very much in love with that girl.

I walk to the central meeting area, greeted by Katheine and coffee.

"Good morning everyone."

"Your Majesty. Did you sleep well?" asks Warren.

"I did. The get-a-way trip was wonderful, but we have work to do now. Any word from Alazaar or the city?"

"None at all," offers Orien as he walks over to join us. "In fact, it's too quiet. We are wondering what he's planning."

"Well, it's for certain that he's planning something. Just because we destroyed his death machine doesn't mean he can't chop off people's heads. He has several executioners with blades to do that, but that's not his style. He is an exhibitionist, not just a murderer. He desires to make a show of his power, so there is no doubt he is planning to do just that."

"I suggest we ride to the mine today and have a look around. See if there is any activity. If there's none, we can gauge the task of removing some rail and cars as we've discussed."

"I'm in," says Ryan.

Camilla says she wants to come too, and of course, Orien is joining.

"Well, none of you are going anywhere till you have breakfast," exclaims Katherine.

"Dear Katherine, we wouldn't think about it," Orien replies.

We all sit down to eat and discuss the latest thoughts about the rail now that the west entrance has been opened.

Afterward, we mount up and ride to Twin Springs.

Meanwhile, Gemma and Alexandra ride into the soldiers camp. Princess Sarah is there to welcome them. As Gemma dismounts, all the men go down on one knee and bow their heads. The most ranking soldier speaks.

"We welcome you Queen Gemma Edmonds. I am Captain Nathan Krytcher, Commander of the regiment. You honor us with your presence in our camp."

Gemma looks around at all the men and grins.

"Well if you're all going to remain on your knees, I'm not apt to learn very much. Please rise, and welcome to our Kingdom. I am eager to learn what you have to teach me."

Princess Sarah then greats Gemma. "Welcome Your Majesty. From what I hear, you're a brave girl and have some experience already."

"Yes, experience at losing and feeling the effects of a sword, Your Royal Highness. I will follow your guidance and learn."

"Such formalities. Please call me Sarah and in this setting I hope it is okay if I call you Gemma?"

"It is absolutely okay Sarah, thank you. Learning the ways of royalty is still something to which I am not accustomed. You too Alexandra, please call me Gemma."

"Just to be clear to my soldiers, Your Majesty, my men and I will refer to you according to your proper title," says the Captain.

"Alexander speaks up. "Okay, let the training begin."

The soldiers fall into formation, knowing what to do.

"Gemma, you may take your place there on the front row. It will seem awkward at first but watch and try to imitate what you see," Alexandra says pointing to an open spot in the front for her.

The men begin a series of exercises and combat moves. It is like watching an Asian dance more than exercise, but Gemma watches and catches on quickly.

As we approach the mine, to our surprise, we hear men chattering. We watch from out of sight to see what we can, back far enough that the horses won't cause a commotion either.

There are a dozen men moving bags, full of presumably Potassium Nitrate, out of the rail cars and onto horse drawn flat wagons. There looks to be about six rail cars at the entrance of the mine. Nearby is a second wagon, packed with bags and already hitched to horses ready to leave.

"So much for seeing the rail and no activity," whispers Ryan.

As we watch, the men push the empty cars inside and take their places on top of the bags on the wagons. A few minutes later both begin to leave. Heading back in the direction of Artems.

"Come on, let's follow them," suggests Orien.

"Indeed, let's go." We return to our horses and stay well behind the two wagons. As they near the city outer edges, they turn down nothing more than a path, leading into the woods. We continue following.

It takes about twenty minutes, but they arrive at a large building. The doors open from within, and the horses, wagons, and people all enter. Then the doors close.

Camilla points to windows high up on the roof. "If we could get up there, we can see inside."

We make our way around to the side and climb up some crates. No one is outside, that we can see anyway, so we make it to the windows without an issue.

Inside we can see several workers unloading the bags from the mine into a large drum. In other drums we can see what we quickly identify as sulfur, and still others ...charcoal. "Alazaar has his own black powder mixing factory here. He has to be supplying ships in return for goods and services, but where is he getting the sulfur?" I think to myself.

We climb back down and make our way back home, talking amongst ourselves as we do.

"With that much black powder we could make a lot of weapons to fight Alazaar's army," says Orien.

Camilla adds, "but we need to find out where the sulfur is coming from. It's certainly not from Westerly, Princess Sarah would not do that to us. Or would she?"

"She absolutely would not. I trust Sarah and her father with my life. But you are correct that we need to know from where it comes. Whoever is supplying Alazaar is no friend to us, meaning we have an unknown enemy. Sarah will know who could be supplying him."

We arrive home safe, but it's early evening already. We laugh that Katherine is going to want to feed us again, and sure enough, we walk into folks having supper.

Amelia comes over to me, "Your Majesty, we have a surprise for the Queen tonight, but we need your help with it."

"Of course. Anything for Gemma. What can I do?"

"It's at your cabin."

"Very well, let's go." We head out to the cavern and over to our cabin. Outside the cabin is a large metal tub.

"We wish to take it inside Your Majesty, so the Queen can bathe in privacy, but we wouldn't enter your residence without you there."

"That is so generous of you all. Gemma will love it. Speaking of Gemma, I wonder what time we might see her return today. I hope she has had a good first day."

"I wouldn't worry about her, Your Majesty. She's a strong woman," says Amelia.

"You are right about that. Come, let's place this inside." Several of us work to maneuver the tub inside and position it in a good spot.

"Now it just needs water. May we fill it now?" Amelia asks.

"I don't see why not. I'll heat up some water when she returns home. I can't tell you all how much this will mean to her. Truly, thank you all very much."

We fill the tub and return to the middle area. Katherine has beer and food for us. A short while later, Sarah, Alexandra, and a very tired Gemma return. Gemma comes and collapses in my lap.

"Hello, my dear, how was your day?" I ask.

"It's been incredible, but I am exhausted."

Sarah laughs. "She did amazing James. She is a real warrior at heart, and we'll give her the skills she's lacking. Tomorrow's a new day, rest up young lady."

190

"James, we're going to return to the camp tonight, there are things Captain Nathan and I are working on. Gemma, we will see you in the morning."

"Sounds good," says Gemma. "Although, I think I've done more running through the forest today, then all my years of running through the forest combined. I may not survive day two," she laughs.

We all laugh, knowing that's not possible. Katherine brings her food, which she happily enjoys.

"So, what did you focus on today Gemma?" I ask.

"We literally ran through the woods all day. I'm not exaggerating. Alexandra is in charge, and she said she wants to see how much stamina I have and how long I can go. I think I did better than she expected."

"I have no doubt you did."

"What have you been doing today James?"

I explain we went to the mine and what we discovered. "I meant to ask Sarah about the sulfur, but I can tomorrow. I knew if Alazaar was being quiet, it was because he is up to something."

"Wow James. If he's got that much explosive, we may need a lot more men." Gemma replies.

"We didn't actually see any stores of explosives, only the manufacturing of it in bulk. I still think he's shipping it to the seaport in exchange for goods and supplies. The Navy ships use lots of black powder onboard for training with the guns."

"That's it! If we can intercept one of those shipments to the port, taking possession of the cargo for our use, it may be enough to give us the edge," says Orien.

"That could actually work. Can we get crews set up to monitor the

191

mine and powder operations a couple of weeks? My guess is shipments are happening on a schedule."

"Absolutely we can," says Warren. "We'll get people on it."

Gemma finishes eating. "That's a great idea gentleman, but if you will excuse me, the activities of the day have left me drained. I think I'm going to retire early tonight."

I offer to escort her to our cabin, and everyone bids us goodnight. We walk to the cabin holding hands and she tells me more about the path they ran and what she saw. As we get to the cabin I tell her that everyone came together while we were away and have a surprise for her inside.

"A surprise? For me? What on earth for?"

I open the door and Gemma walks in.

"James Edmonds, you knew about this?" She yells and hugs me, seeing the tub.

"No no, this wasn't me my love. This was Amelia, Abbie, your Mom, and several others again. They all love you. It was a surprise to me as well. I simply helped them bring it in the room."

"I can heat up some water for you darling."

Gemma strips naked and climbs in. "Maybe a little, but this feels wonderful. It sure beats the river. Oh wow! James did you thank them for me?"

I put a pail of water on the fire that I started earlier, and let it begin to heat up. "Yes my dear, I thanked them many times."

Gemma is splashing and enjoying the water. "This is the second time I've been able to bathe indoors since I've met you James. Only this time, will you join me? There is plenty of room."

"Let me warm up the water for us and I'd love too."

It doesn't take long and the water in the pail is boiling. I carry it to the tub carefully and begin to pour. "Say when to stop. We don't want it too hot."

Gemma mixes up the water with her legs, laughing like a kid the whole time. It doesn't take too much boiling water to raise the temperature to steamy.

I set the pail back by the fireplace, strip off my clothes and join her in the water. Our lips melt together as we embrace each other. Steam rises off the water and our bodies, as we lay there arm in arm, kissing, caressing, and getting aroused in the romantic glow of the fire.

"You are so soft. Your skin is like silk," I caress her arm, pouring water over her shoulder out of my hand. I touch her face, and her lips, feeling the sensuality of her body. She lays her head on my shoulder.

"I love you James."

"I love you too Gemma."

"Oh, heavens I do not want to get out of this tub, but I really am tired and looking forward to more training tomorrow."

She climbs out, dries off and crawls under blankets. I follow, only stopping to add a couple logs to the fire. Then we snuggle and kiss, and she falls asleep quickly on my arm. I just lay there, looking at her, feeling things I've never experienced before. She is everything.

Gemma's Training

Gemma gets up well before sunrise the next morning. She kisses James while he sleeps and rides off to the soldier's camp. Upon arriving she is once again greeted by Alexandra, who's waiting on her.

"Good morning Alexandra. What do we work on today? How long till we're working with swords?"

Alexandra laughs. "Swords? You have much to learn before you can think about swords. First we train your body. Then we train your mind. Then we can think about weapons. But these, right here," she points to Gemma's hands and her head. "These are your greatest weapons, and you must learn to control them first. So, we will focus on that over the next two weeks and see how you do."

Two weeks? Gemma thinks to herself. She's disappointed but she trusts Alexandra.

"Yesterday we were easy on you. Each day will get harder. I will make you push yourself to your breaking point. Your muscles will hurt. Your mind will betray you. I will break you down and rebuild you. Forget what you think you know about fighting. It will only cloud your judgement. But I know you can do this."

We start by running, and then more running. Then we exercise with the men. Alexandra fills my pockets and a backpack with rocks. We go up hills, over rough terrain, and Gemma gets scraped and bruised after she takes a couple tumbles. But she remains strong and dedicated. By the end of the day, she is again worn out.

Alexandra tells her, "Gemma, you are free to return to your home each night, but I want to challenge you that starting tomorrow, you remain here until your training is complete. I know you love James, but right now he is a distraction. You need to focus."

"Remain here for how long?" Gemma stops to think. Leaving James for an extended period is not something she considered. But after giving it some thought, she realizes Alexandra is right. "I understand, and I will speak with him about it tonight. Thank you Alexandra."

Gemma returns home for the evening, thinking about what Alexandra said. Being away from James for a long period will be difficult, but she's determined to follow Alexandra's advice, trusting in her experience.

She arrives back at the cabin at dark. She ate dinner with the soldiers, so she is free to rest now. Upon entering the cabin, I am there and jump up at the site of seeing her for the first time today. I welcome her with a hug and a kiss.

"Greetings my love. How was your day today?" I ask.

"It was hard. Not as much running as yesterday, but still, lots of exercise. Alexandra suggests that I remain there for the duration of my training, rather than coming home each evening." Tears form in her eyes.

"Remain there? For how long? I can understand how that could be better for you, although I would surely miss you. What do you want to do?"

"I don't know. I really want to focus but the thought of being away from you for several weeks is depressing."

I pull her close and kiss her. "You know I love you, and I will hate being away from you too. But, I also sense, deep down, you want this. And I think traveling between here and there each day is taking valuable time and energy. You know I love sharing at the end of each day about our day, but I'm not going anywhere. I promise you I will be here when your training is complete."

Gemma kisses me passionately, pressing her body into mine. "You know me so well. So, you think it's a good idea."

"I do. You're going across the river, not across the Kingdom. If you had to be here, you could be. I will miss you, but the men and I are going to be doing some traveling the next few weeks as well tracking down Alazaar's supplier of sulfur. It might be the perfect time and allow you to concentrate on learning everything you can."

"You're so supportive. And you're correct. I will miss you."

"I will miss you as well, but we have a lifetime to share afterward. Now come, the water is warm. Relax while you can."

We get in the water, and she lays against me. "This is so nice. I will miss this too," she says.

"Yes, you will miss this more than me." I start to laugh. She smacks my chest, laughing.

"You know better."

The next morning, I get up with her. "I have to speak with Sarah, so I will accompany you to camp this morning my dear."

"That would be wonderful. Our last few moments together, before life takes us away."

We ride to camp. As we approach someone announces, "His Majesty the King is here."

Everyone again goes to one knee. Princess Sarah comes forth from her tent.

"James. This is unexpected. Did you come to train with Gemma?" She smiles knowing I wouldn't do that.

I laugh. "No, I couldn't handle the embarrassment of her making me look bad each day."

"I need to speak with you Sarah about business matters if you have time."

Alexandra calls for Gemma.

"Goodbye James. I will see you in a few weeks I guess." Gemma kisses me goodbye and begins walking toward Alexandra.

"Have fun my love. You can send for me if needed, but I'm sure you'll be fine. I love you."

"I love you too James."

"Don't worry James, we'll take good care of her. She a natural leader and fighter, Alexandra will teach her much," says Sarah.

"Come, let's talk," she adds.

We walk inside a big tent with tables and chairs, and coffee. "Want some?" she asks.

"I would love some."

I inform Sarah about what we found at the mine, and the factory, then ask her about other sulfur suppliers.

Sarah thinks and nods her head. "This is certainly interesting news. The next closest sulfur mine is the Blue Ridge mine on the western seaboard. That means he's paying a heavy cost for transportation to his plant. I wonder how he made contact with them?"

"No doubt through merchants in the markets at Artems. He is probably blackmailing someone. I will send word to Mark to see what he can learn. Seems someone in the market is more loyal to Alazaar than myself."

"If you find out anything, please let me know."

"And please don't worry about Gemma. Alexandra is tough, but she won't let her get hurt."

"Thanks, I appreciate it, and I appreciate you coming to us with your men to help. We may have a reprieve from Alazaar's anger, but it won't last forever."

"We're glad to be here James. Please, come visit again soon."

"I will."

I return to the cavern.

Gemma meets up with Alexander ready to begin her training. "What's on my agenda today," she asks.

"You know the drill. First we run."

Today two of the men join us, and the four of us take off to the top of range nearby. Two hours later, we stop on top and overlook the area.

"Alright Gemma let's see what you're made of. Charles is going to begin working with you in hand-to-hand combat." Charles stands looking at Gemma.

Gemma looks at Charles. He's a least 6'5" tall and 250 pounds. "Him? You want me to learn to fight him?"

"You won't learn much fighting a child. Charles is an excellent teacher."

Gemma greets Charles.

"Your Majesty, it is an honor to work with you. My job is to teach you, not hurt you."

"Very well, let's begin." Charles takes a fighting stance and begins instructing Gemma about how to holds one's hand, how to throw punches, how to block, and how to use her smaller frame and agility to take on an opponent the size of Charles.

Every day for the next two weeks is the same. Physical endurance exercise and person to person combat skills. Gemma becomes stronger and faster each day. After two weeks, she's nowhere near as tired each night.

"You've done well in two weeks Gemma." Alexandra encourages her.

"But two weeks only introduces you to the moves. It will take years to master them. You must continue learning what we teach you your entire life."

"Starting tomorrow we will begin using the bow and arrow. Have you used bows and arrows?"

"Oh yes, to hunt as a child and young adult. I feel very comfortable with them for hunting. But not as a weapon."

"You will learn the difference. When hunting more often than not your prey is standing still. When fighting either you or your opponent is moving. Have you used a bow and arrow while riding a horse?"

"No. I have not."

Two more weeks of training ensues. Charles and Gemma spar daily. There is always running, and tactics to learn. Gemma is fitted with a bow to her size and arm length. She is taught about bow cords, and which woods are best for the bow vs the arrows. Already knowing wood is a huge plus for her.

She starts stationary shooting. Then she begins training while riding. First on the back of a horse with Alexander. She focuses on balance and loading the weapon while holding on with her knees. She's excited when she gets to try solo riding.

"Can I go and get my own horse? I think it would better to train with my horse."

"We will send a rider to get your horse. That is a fantastic idea Gemma." replies Alexandra.

Gemma is delighted to receive her horse, Caspian, the next day. He has been hers for several years. The white and brown spots give the stallion character. Caspian is fast and strong, and the two share a strong bond together.

Training commences with Caspian. Alexandra is very impressed with how well Gemma is learning. Gemma is also proud. She can feel she is stronger, faster, and more agile than she was. Sparring with Charles has been excellent training. She no longer fears the idea of a larger opponent.

Week five begins. After the morning run and sparring session, Alexandra draws a sword.

"You've done very, very well Gemma. Your dedication has been exemplary. You've even given my men motivation to become better warriors. Between you and me, you're better than most of them already. Now, what's the first rule we taught you?" That's the most important.

"Never ever underestimate your opponent." Gemma replies.

"Exactly. And never judge by size." Alexandra retorts.

"Today we begin training with the sword. Like one-on-one combat, there are steps and techniques to master. From basic cuts to parrying and blocking. Using feints, deceiving your opponent by pretending to strike in one direction, then changing to another, and repostes, a counterattack following a parry, using an opening provided to gain the advantage. Even disarming your opponent is possible."

"But in two weeks, you will just barely scratch the surface. James is an excellent swordsman, though he doesn't admit it. I hope you and he will continue your practice together throughout your life."

"I'm sure he would love that as much as I would."

"Very well, let's get started."

The final two weeks of Gemma's training goes very fast. She continues to work hard. But she is also excited that soon she can be reunited with James. She doesn't have a great deal of time to think about the community, but at night she sheds a few tears of loneliness.

The final couple of days, Gemma is introduced to training and fighting as a team. She is very much a natural leader as Alexandra foresaw. The men have no issues taking orders from her.

The last day, Charles and a few other men approach Gemma.

"Your Majesty. It has been our greatest honor to work with you these past weeks. You have incredible strength and endurance, and we would all follow you onto any battlefield."

Gemma breaks protocol and hugs Charles. "I shall never forget you, nor be able to repay you for all your patience and challenges with me. You are a good man Charles. I shall miss you."

With that Gemma mounts her horse and bids everyone goodbye.

Sarah waves, "Tell James we will be in touch."

"I will," she yells as she rides away,

Strategic Destruction

The men and women of the community have setup schedules to keep an eye on the mine, and the comings and goings around the explosives factory.

It's been hard not having Gemma here and I miss her terribly. But I know she is in good hands and needs the training with Alexandra and the soldiers much more than these days with me.

I report back to the group what Sarah told me about sulfur coming in from the west, and we've been able to confirm that is happening through our surveillance.

It's been two weeks since Gemma left, and we observed one large shipment of sulfur being received into the factory. With the shipments coming from the west, it complicates being able to intercept it. The route is on the far side of Artems, and through areas not as well known to us. We've been working to develop plans as how to proceed.

Over morning coffee, I speak with Orien.

"We need to talk with Mark and learn about this sulfur supplier. Nothing moves in and out of Artems without his knowledge. Since we're aware of only one shipment in two weeks, we have some time. We can only hope that the next shipment arrives next week on the same day. With a little luck we can schedule an intercept with some accuracy."

"The men watching the mine have concluded that the mine is only being used three days a week. It makes sense they are getting all the saltpeter they need for so few sulfur shipments. That also provides a large window for us to get in, get what we need, and get out." Orien responds.

"True, my only concern is timing. If we tip our hand at the mine before the next shipment of sulfur, the sulfur may not come. And likewise, if we steal the sulfur first, Alazaar may heavily increase the security around the mine. It would be best to hit them both the same day."

"Two teams again? We should be able to make that happen," Warren adds.

"We need to see if that sulfur shows up next Wednesday. That will be two weeks. If so, we could set a plan with some certainty to attack two weeks from that date."

"The mine will be easy if no one is there that day. Both rail and cars are easily accessible from the entrance," says Warren.

Orien adds, "better still. They have what they need stored at the front of the entrance. If we remove stuff from the second or third level, what we take may go unnoticed for a period of time."

"That's a perfect idea. We can start extracting stuff next week, and it's doubtful anyone will notice."

"But first we have to talk to Mark. Who's up for another trip to Artems?"

Several volunteer, so we schedule a trip the next day.

It's always great to see Mark.

"Your Majesty! My friend James, you will not begrudge me being informal will you? I still can't believe it. You are now King! I am friends with the King. Oh, but we loved your father. You know this. Still, I did not know him personally. But you James, we can tell stories together, yes?"

He starts dancing around singing some silly song, doing his best to embarrass me.

"Are you done?" I ask laughing at him.

He just waves and keeps dancing. So, I sit down and motion for a beer.

"Here you are Your Majesty. My name is Mary, can I get you anything else?" asks the waitress.

"Can you get him to sit down before he hurts himself?" I ask, laughing loudly.

"Forgive me Your Majesty, but no one has the skills to make Mark do anything," she laughs.

Actually, it is good to see people happy and dancing. Others join in with Mark. I enjoy the beer and chat with Orien.

Eventually Mark comes over and huffs down, out of breath. "So,

James, what brings you back to my humble domain?"

"I have reason to believe that the Blue Ridge Mine is supplying Alazaar with sulfur. Would you know anything about that?"

"Sulfur now? What would he be doing with sulfur?"

"We found a factory where he's mixing black powder using saltpeter from Twin Springs and sulfur from the west, then shipping it to the eastern ports. Princess Sarah of Westerly is not supplying him of course, so the only other supplier she could think of is the Blue Ridge Mine."

"That be a long way away. It's possible. Let me ask around and I can find out what the word is. I can have someone fetch Derrick; he would know. Mary, go and fetch Derrick to come and speak with us."

A short while later, Mary returns with Derrick. She walks over to us and introduces Derrick to the King.

"Your Majesty, it is an honor to meet you. How may I help?"

Mark speaks up. "Derrick, what do you know of sulfur being shipped here from the western ports?

Derrick looks around covering his mouth with his finger, signaling for quiet. Mark looks at me, noting the fear in Derrick's eyes.

I ask, "Derrick, tell us what you know."

Mark motions that we move upstairs to speak more openly. With that we move upstairs.

Upstairs, Derrick begins. "I am aware of what you ask. If I am seen speaking of it, it will bring death to my family. I'm sorry Your Majesty, please forgive me if I have betrayed our Kingdom. They came to me, asking me to make contact with my suppliers. Are they using it for nefarious purposes?"

"Calm down Derrick, you've done nothing wrong. I understand the times we live in and what is required to protect those we love. So far as we can tell, the sulfur is being used to make black powder and being shipped to the eastern ports for use on sea ships."

Orien speaks up, "We desire to intercept a shipment of his sulfur. Can you tell us how often he receives it?"

"Yes, yes. Every other Wednesday a shipment arrives by way of the Eastern Caravans. But they are very heavily guarded. What you suggest will not be an easy task."

Orien says to me, "When we saw them unloading the sulfur at the factory, there were very few guards. Perhaps the shipment is only escorted to the city."

"That's possible. The caravans continue onward east to other cities. They would not want to lose the time guarding sulfur once in Artems," adds Derrick.

"Nor would Alazaar wish to draw unnecessary attention to his activities. This is good, meaning we could possibly intercept next week's shipment."

"That's very possible Your Majesty. We could break into the factory after dark and take what we need."

I contemplate the various scenarios in my head as I listen to the men talk. "This is fantastic information Derrick. Your secrets are safe with us. And on behalf of the entire Kingdom, I thank you for your loyalty. We will be rid of Alazaar in time, and your family will be safe."

"Thank you Your Majesty, thank you so much. Mark, if ever I can..."

Mark interrupts him, "I know Derrick. Thank you for helping us. Now exit through the kitchen so no one sees you please. We'll be in touch my friend."

He bows to me and leaves.

"That's exactly the information we needed. Mark, you're amazing. I may have to formally Knight you someday."

"Me, a Knight? Who could imagine such a thing? Just stay my friend James."

"Always, my good man. Always."

With the knowledge we have, we bid farewell and return home. My mind is filled with thoughts of Gemma as I ride, and how she would love to be with us.

Upon our return home, we begin thinking of how to break into the factory. If done well, the soldiers will just think it's vagrants having fun and nothing more.

With a week before the next shipment, we focus our efforts on obtaining rail and cars from the mine. Again, working under the cover of darkness, and taking the extra time to retrieve stuff from the lower levels, the chances of anything being found missing is slim.

By the end of the week, we have several cars, and enough rail to begin a line into the cavern. We can get more in the coming weeks.

The next Wednesday arrives, and we have our plan to raid the black powder factory. In addition to rail from the mine, we picked up several bags of saltpeter as well.

What sulfur we get tonight won't shutdown Alazaar's operation, but it will allow us to mix our own batch of explosives for use in the near future.

We arrive at the factory, and everything is quiet. There seems to be one guard patrolling outside. We make fast work of knocking him unconscious and lifting the keys from his belt.

Erik climbed up and looked through the window. He gives a thumbs up to make our entry.

Upon entering, as we'd hoped, the newly delivered sulfur is stacked up in bags on the wagon. We begin loading it on our wagon. Then proceed to acquire some black powder bags since they're easily available. After thirty minutes, we have a load. Erik and Orien take off with the wagon. I use branches to hide the tracks of the wheels and take off to join them. That went really well.

The next couple of weeks we focus heavily on making weapons and explosive charges. We plan to blow up Alazaar's factory and collapse the entrance of the mine. After Gemma's return, we will begin the final battle to defeat Alazaar.

We make bombs, and charges to use against Alazaar's army, in addition to bows, arrows, and swords. But first, we need to destroy his defenses.

With Sarah's men here, plus our own, we are two hundred plus going against five hundred plus. We hope the explosives provide adequate advantage.

Ryan comes in, "We've prepared what we need to blow the mine and the factory. We just need to set a date Your Majesty."

"We must now wait for Gemma's return. After we blow the factory, it will be time to advance on the castle. And we can't do that without Gemma."

"Understood. So, we wait."

Chapter TEN: Our Heroine

Gemma Returns

"Good morning Your Majesty. Are you feeling well this morning?" asks Katherine.

"I am indeed. I believe we are close to the final faceoff with Alazaar in the coming weeks, but I pray daily for Gemma's return. Her absence has been hard. I'm excited for her to see and hear of all that's been done. I'm sure she has learned much, so I am also yearning to hear of her tales."

"We all miss Gemma very much. To have her laughter and charms fill this chamber again.... oh, but don't you worry. Gemma is a strong girl. She will return when she is ready. If anything had happened, they would let us know."

"I know she will, and you are correct, nothing has happened to her."

Around midday I am assisting with our weapons storage. We built a building not far from the front of the cave, leaving the west entrance clear for lumber operations. We've accumulated a large supply of various artifacts to use, hopefully, in the near future.

As I carry a bundle of arrow shafts I hear my name being called. "James! James!"

I turn and see Gemma riding into our camp.

"Gemma!!"

Gemma rides in, jumps from her horse and runs into my arms. Our bodies embrace. Our lips melt together. My arms pull her so tight to my body I feel I will break her. Her arms are tight around me. Time once more stops, as the love explodes in my heart.

"Oh James, I've missed you. I love you so much."

I step back from our embrace, "Let me just look at you."

We just gaze into each other's eyes for minutes. Her smile is extraordinary, her hair longer than ever, tears of happiness streaming down her face.

"You're back! O Gemma I love you; I can't believe you're home. I've missed you too."

I lift her up in my arms and we spin and dance in happiness. I just keep kissing her. She laughs with such joy.

"Gemma!!" Madeline screams and runs to Gemma. Erik is not far behind.

I set her down. "Mom!" she shrieks as she embraces her mom. Erik embraces both of them.

Word spreads quickly of her return, and everyone comes to welcome her home. Applause, cheers, clapping, and laughter roar through the forest.

Madeline steps back. "Gemma! Look at you. You've gained weight! Look at the muscles in your arms. You look amazing dear child."

"Thanks mom. I am stronger, and healthier than ever in my life. I have so many things to tell you. I've missed all of you so much."

I put my arm around her waist, standing next to her, she is much stouter for sure.

"You're more beautiful than ever Gemma," I tell her.

She leans over and kisses me, while others now make their way for hugs and bows to the Queen. She takes the time to speak with each and every one of them.

Speech, speech, speech, chants the crowd.

Gemma steps up on the old tree stump once more, overlooking all those she loves, she says...

"My friends. My family. Your welcoming is more than any girl could ask for. I do love each and every one of you, and I thank you all for your love and support. You truly will never know how much that drove me each day of these last six weeks. But I would be so remiss if I do not publicly thank my dearest and closest supporter, my beloved husband and King, James."

"James, from the day you saved me, you have given me hope, encouragement, love, and guidance. There has not been a single day that I have not thought of you. It was knowing that when I return, I will stand stronger by your side as we fight for our Kingdom and our future. My love for you will never end my beloved husband."

The crowd cheers again. Gemma looks at me as she steps down. I reach out and take her hand to help her. She steps down into my arms. "I love you." I say again to her.

"I love you too my dear."

She smiles and looks around. "Well, I want to hear about and see everything that has happened in my absence," she remarks.

I take her arm, and we begin to walk to the cavern. Her eyes get huge when she sees the open west entrance, complete with rail, and new buildings. Outside the staging platform for trees and sawing prep.

We continue on to the weapons storage. She is totally amazed. She inspects our work and craftsmanship.

"Well done you all."

Rachel asks, "Did you learn how to fight, and how to make weapons?"

"I learned we are always learning how to fight, and how we improve our minds. And yes, how to make weapons."

"Are our weapons good?" Rachel asks.

"Your weapons are very good Rachel. You all have done well. But I might be able to teach you ways to make them better." Gemma grins.

"Can you teach us to fight too?"

"I certainly can, but first we have a lot of work to do."

Rachel nods and runs to her friends.

"This all is really truly amazing you all. You should be very proud," she says.

"We are all so proud of you Gemma. I am proud of you," I reply.

As we begin walking back to the cave, Princess Sarah and Alexandra ride in.

Gemma greets them. "Why did you not ride in with me earlier if you wished to visit? You know you are always welcome."

"And take away from your return welcoming?" Sarah replies. "No, you deserve the welcoming on your own."

They dismount and walk over. A couple young men step forward, "We will tend to your horses my lady."

Gemma thanks them.

"Hello James. I can't tell you how much we enjoyed you sharing your lovely wife with us these past weeks. She is a true fighter. Now it is up to you to continue her training."

"I fear Sarah, that she will now be teaching me." I laugh as Gemma blushes.

Come let us go inside and have a beer. We walk into the cave and sit at the table. Katherine brings wine and beer for us to choose from.

"So, is this a social visit," I ask.

"Not entirely James. I have received word that my father is sending an additional one-hundred men, as is the Kingdom of Swallows. My father and King Richmond of Swallows are friends, and we all want to assist you in your fight here against Alazaar. We have heard he has as many as five-hundred men, and if we don't stop him soon, none of our Kingdoms are safe."

"Two-hundred more men are coming? That is fantastic news," says Orien.

"That is extremely good news," adds Gemma. "Now we should be very prepared for Alazaar."

"Thank you for bringing us this news Sarah. We will eagerly await their arrival."

"They should be here by week's end," she adds.

"James, the number one rule I've learned these past weeks is to never underestimate your enemy. We must assume that Alazaar's men are fiercely loyal and will fight to the death. He rewards them handsomely for their loyalty," says Gemma.

"You are correct, Gemma. The skirmishes we've faced up till now have been nothing compared to what we will face soon. More people will die. But, in the end, we will honor their sacrifice."

We spend the next few hours going over everything we've learned, and Gemma shares with us everything that she learned.

"Be proud of her James. She worked hard overcoming her fears, and challenging men twice her size. She has the heart of a warrior, and the admiration of all my soldiers," says Sarah.

"I am very proud of her, and it is evident she has studied and worked hard."

Katherine comes from the cooking area. "I hope everyone is hungry. I made your favorite meal Gemma, in celebration of your return to us. We have much to be happy about."

"Oh Katherine, you are so good to me. I won't take away from the cooks at your camp Sarah, but their skills are nothing compared to Katherine's ways in a kitchen. I am so grateful to enjoy your meals again dear Katherine."

Everyone laughs as helpers bring out the feast. Roasted wild turkeys, with plenty of vegetables, potatoes, and sweets to savor. The aroma is heavenly and fills the entire room as food is placed on tables.

I stand and lift my drink. "A toast my friends, to my beloved wife and your Queen. Gemma, you have returned safely to us. Stronger, wiser, and with great confidence in yourself. A young woman left us, but a warrior woman has returned to us. I love you with all my heart. TO GEMMA!"

"TO GEMMA!" The community echoes.

"Thank you James," Gemma says to me as she blushes being the center of attention.

After dinner, Gemma and I stand and greet those around us. Soon she asks, "James, can we retire early this evening? I would like to relax with you in our cabin, and I look forward to sleeping in a real bed once more. You have spoiled me James with luxury but allow me this one endearment – a hot bath."

"Of course, my love. Shall we head there now? No one will begrudge you some rest after all you have given."

I stand and take Gemma's hand. We bid our 'good evenings', and 'good nights' to those around, and walk to our cabin. Once there I pick her up in my arms, sweeping her literally off her feet, and carry her inside.

"James! You silly, romantic, adorable man. I am so happy to be back with you." She looks around the room. "And so happy to be back with this tub. May we make use of it again?"

"Of course we can my dear. I did not know when to expect you, but your friends have stayed diligent each day to replace the water, keeping it fresh."

Gemma collapses on the bed as I start a fire in the fireplace, and shortly thereafter I am dumping hot water into the tub. Once Gemma sees the steam rising from the water, she stands. I walk to her and unbutton her shirt, gazing into her eyes as I do. She smiles and lets me undress her. I kiss each part of her as her body becomes more visible in front of me. Her muscles are much more clearly defined. Her abdomen tight, her breasts firm. Even the muscles in her thighs are noticeable stronger.

I undress myself under her watchful gaze. Then we melt into each other. Hugging, kissing, caressing, enjoying the warmth and feel of our skin pressed against each other. I help her to the tub, and we climb in. The water is toasty warm and Gemma slides completely under the water. She pops up a minute later, wiping the water off her face and pulling back her hair. She smiles and giggles noticing I'm staring at her.

"Oh, this feels amazing. Thank you James. For everything, but mostly for believing in me. I was scared when I left for training. Even knowing you were only a short ride away, the thought of not seeing you for such a long time terrified me. I cried, at night, at first, but as the training got harder, I found myself more relaxed and more exhausted. Everyone treated me with such kindness, it was an experience I shall never forget. Thank you for supporting me."

I sit in the water, facing her, running my fingers through her hair and caressing her cheek and feeling her tender lips with my fingers. "You are so courageous Gemma. Not many women could do what you have done."

She blushes again and leans her head on my shoulder as we just hold each other. Words are not necessary; we get lost in each other in the moment.

Later, we move to the bed and passion takes over. Our bodies become one, our arms wrapped tightly around each other as our tongues dance to the cadence of our own rhythm.

The next morning Gemma is resting her head on my chest.

"James?" she asks.

"Yes dear."

"We may have made a baby last night."

"A baby? Seriously? Are you.... ? When will you know?"

"Would that disappoint you?"

"Absolutely NOT! That would not disappoint me at all. Don't say such a thing. A baby? Wow."

She rolls over and looks in my eyes. "I won't know for several weeks. I'm just thinking about what it will be like to have a family with you."

"Do you want that?" I ask, caressing her cheek.

"Yes James, I want that very much."

"So do I my love, so do I."

"Oh, I could just lay here all day.... with you," she says.

"That day will come my dear, but we have much work to do. Let's go."

We get up, clean up and make our way to the community area. It is a beautiful day outside.

Gemma stretches, "I feel guilty for sleeping in after six weeks of hard training. I can't stop with the exercises they taught me just because I'm back. I will get lazy fast."

"You deserve to have slept in this morning. You worked hard, and you're not going to quit. Really I should exercise with you."

"Sarah told me you are an excellent swordsman, although you won't admit it. She said I should ask you to finish my training."

"Perhaps that would be good for us," I respond.

We join the group for breakfast, with more talk of the last few weeks.

More importantly now, is that we turn our attention to the coming weeks.

The Battle Commences

Several days later the additional soldiers arrive and join the camp. Gemma and I work closely with Sarah and Alexandra, to get everyone settled. A few days after that, we have all the logistics worked out and everyone feels at home.

The four of us, along with Captain Krytcher, Orien and Ryan meet each morning going over maps and details of the best way to approach our offense against Alazaar. Most of his men are based at the castle, his way of ensuring he is well guarded at all times. But we have also received word of other small outposts along the trade routes that have soldiers loyal to Alazaar.

This morning, we are in Sarah's main tent, discussing the best use of the explosives we've manufactured when we hear screams coming from across the river - back at the cave. We run to our horses as a rider storms towards us from across the river.

"Soldiers Your Majesty. They have found us, lots of them, attacking us at the cave."

Captain Krytcher blows the trumpet. "Mount your horses, we are being attacked, it's time to fight."

Gemma and I are already across the river followed by Alexandra and a dozen men. At the cave is complete chaos. Maybe seventy-five to eighty soldiers have attacked. The battle begins. Swords clash, arrows fly, and men fall. Ours and theirs.

Gemma's training comes back to her immediately. She is best with her bow, which she keeps on her horse. She rides well and shoots straight. I attack those inside the cavern with my sword from my horse.

Within minutes the other soldiers all join in the fight. It's no match for Alazaar's soldiers against the three hundred men we have from allies. A few minutes later dead bodies lay everywhere. There is weeping in the cavern. Gemma and I ride side by side, taking in the carnage. We could not get there fast enough, and lost men and women.

"There is a survivor." Gemma points and jumps from her horse. She runs to the young man and lifts him to her shoulder. He has been stabbed, and bleeding profusely. Gemma applies first aid to stop the bleeding and consoles him. "Who are you?" she asks.

"I am Gerard, of the 123rd infantry regiment of the Kingdom of Swallows. I am pleased to be here."

Gerard is about 27 years old and handsome. He has black hair and looks debonair in his military uniform. The is wound is severe.

"You're going to be okay. Keep pressure on your wound with this bandage," she tells him knowing that she is not qualified to do more for him in his condition. "Medics will be here, stay strong." She wipes the sweet from his forehead and helps him rest upon a rock.

Others are laying around, but now soldiers are here helping the injured. Gemma walks back to her horse as I ride over to her.

"Are you okay?" I ask.

"Yes James, I'm okay," she says as tears run down her face. "How are you?"

"I'm fine. Your parents are in the communal area. They are both fine as well."

"Thank you James."

Gemma mounts her horse, and we ride to the front outside the cave entrance. Sarah and Alexandra are there, mounted on horses as well.

Sarah says, "I'm sorry James. Word is you have lost eight people. Six men and two women. What kind of barbarians kill unarmed helpless women in a raid?"

"Barbarians! You said it right Sarah," Gemma responds.

Alexandra speaks up. "I saw your training in use already Gemma. You fought well."

"Thanks to you and Charles. I have much more respect now for all brave men in our Army. I realize it's not just wielding weapons and he who is strongest wins."

Alexandra nods. We ride to the front and tie off the horses. Most of the soldiers have returned to camp. We enter the cave. Madeline sees us. "Gemma." She walks over and hugs her daughter. "Praise be, you're okay child."

"I'm okay mom. The training was so beneficial, I killed four men. That was the first time I've taken a life. I understand now, in defense of the innocent, sometimes it must be done."

Orien asks, "Your Majesty, what now?"

"Now we fight back. We take the fight to Artems and the mine. Now we load Alazaar's dead soldiers on a wagon and return them to him. I'm going to have it delivered to his courtyard."

"James is that wise?" asks Gemma.

"It is time Gemma. We have the men, we have the explosives, and I will not bury one more of our community because of that man."

"Orien, Sarah, tomorrow we attack, we start with the mine, then we hit the factory, and then we attack the castle. I want twenty with us at the mine, and to attack the factory. Sarah, please have your men near the gates of Artems by noon tomorrow. I will join with you after disposing of the mine and factory. Then we attack the castle together."

"Yes James, we'll be there."

"Orien, will you please oversee the loading of Alazaar's men. Ryan, we need to bring everything we have tomorrow. Gemma, will you and Alexandra ensure the army has whatever they need please."

"Tomorrow we take back our Kingdom."

Everyone nods and cheers. Gemma hugs me and heads off with Alexandra and Captain Krytcher. I coordinate with the teams to finalize our plans.

Sarah takes my hand. "Today you truly acted as King. I'm so proud of you and how you took control. The whole community and my soldiers respect you. Soon, the entire Kingdom will respect you."

"Thank you Sarah. I wish we had more time, but we just don't. We are ready, and with Gemma by my side, I feel we must do this now."

Sarah squeezes my hand, "I agree with you James."

By evening everything is set. I tell everyone, "We leave at dawn."

Gemma returns a short while later. "All the soldiers are ready. The men are well armed and have been briefed as to the layout of the castle. Everyone is ready James. I am ready too, to stand by your side and fight or die with you."

"My beloved Gemma. I find such strength in your courage. If I die tomorrow, know that I died loving you."

"Dear James," she says, looking in my eyes, "if you die, I die."

We kiss each other and I fill her in on what the agenda for tomorrow is. Afterward she asks, "one last walk by the river darling?"

"Absolutely my dear." I put my arm around her, and we head down by the water.

Morning comes. Gemma and I open the door to leave our cabin. Outside stands the whole community. They begin to chant, "Long Live the King. Long Live the Queen."

I raise my hands to quiet them down.

"Thank you all. On behalf of Gemma and myself, we love you all. Today will have its challenges, but we've already overcome so many challenges together. Today we will see the end of Alazaar's rule."

Everyone applauds as we mount our horses and prepare to leave. We head out to meet the others. Sarah and Alexandra are out front and ride over to us, behind them stands the soldiers. Three hundred of them.

Off to the side are two wagons, piled high with dead soldiers.

Coming out of the cavern is the twenty-person team going with us to the mine, led by Orien and Ryan.

I ask Gemma, "Are we ready?"

"We are Your Majesty."

Then I ask Sarah, "Are we ready?"

"We are Your Majesty."

"Very well, we will be at the Gates of the Castle at noon."

"We will be there James."

I raise my sword in the air. "TO VICTORY."

"TO VICTORY," everyone shouts back.

We ride out toward the mine. Our pace is faster than usual to make sure we can meet our schedule.

When we arrive near the mine we see and hear a couple men working, but it's quiet otherwise.

Orien asks, "How do you want to do this?"

"We're going in the front door Orien. You come with me."

"Gemma, hold everyone else here until we eliminate these two."

She nods.

Orien and I ride up to the men. Two additional men walk out of the mine.

I shout to them, "Greetings, we're from the north on our way to Artems. We didn't know this was a working mine."

The man in front replies, "This mine is under the operation of Alazaar. Be on your way."

I dismount my horse, "My friend, may we water our horses, we have traveled far?"

Acting naive I ask, "So what do they mine here? This is a large mine?

"I said be on your way," says the front man again. He draws his sword and points it at me. I raise my hands, "good man, I just wish to water my horse."

The man loses his patience and charges me. In an instance as he closes in I thrust my sword into his chest. Orien attacks the worker nearest him. Then he dismounts, and we make quick work overpowering the remaining two men.

Gemma and the others, seeing us in a fight rush to our aid, but we have it handled.

"Wow James, nicely done," she says.

Ryan gets to work setting charges. We wish to completely seal the mine at this time. We can dig it back out someday in the future when we have the Kingdom again. For now, there will be no more explosives made from our saltpeter.

"The charges are ready," shouts Ryan.

We all move back. "Make it happen Ryan," I yell.

Ryan pushes the plunger, and an explosion rocks the mine. The entrance fully collapses and a good portion of the mountain falls in front of it.

Everyone cheers.

"Perfect! Now let's go do it again at the factory."

We leave and head to the factory only a short distance away. Arriving there, we can see noticeably more security.

Gemma asks, "the direct approach again?"

"Yes my Queen. Only this time we all go."

"Is everyone ready? LET'S FIGHT!" I scream.

We all ride fast directly toward the soldiers. Swords clash and Gemma puts her bow and arrows to use again. The soldiers drop fast, the fight only lasting a few minutes as twenty take on only twelve.

"You're really good at riding and using your bow Gemma. You learned that in two weeks?"

"All I had to learn was how to balance James, I've been hunting since I was a child with a bow and arrow. And that custom bow they built to fit my arm length; I didn't know of such things, but it makes all the difference."

"I'm impressed."

"Ryan, you're up."

We walk inside. There is a considerable amount of black powder that's ready to ship. Ryan laughs out loud.

"Oh, Your Majesty, when this place blows, they're going to hear it at the castle. They may even see it too. This is going to make a huge fireball."

Ryan is giddy with excitement. I chuckle at his amusement.

"It's in your hands my friend, do it."

Ryan takes charge and in about twenty minutes, the charges are ready.

"Everyone back up, we're going to announce our arrival to Alazaar."

We back way far away.

3, 2, 1. Ryan pushes the plunger. The explosion is so loud, and the fireball rises so far in the air, everyone in Artems hears and sees it.

Alazaar runs to the balcony. "Guards, prepare for attack." He looks to the north and immediately knows his factory is gone. He his furious. Morena, Morena!, we're under attack."

Our team rapidly rides to the Castle and meets up with Sarah. I jump from my horse and run to a wagon piled with the dead soldiers. I climb on top and raise my sword in the air.

"LET'S RIDE." Sarah, Alexandra, and a dozen soldiers storm the gate of the castle. The wagon plows through behind them.

I scream, "ALAZAAR! ALAZAAR! ALAZAAR! YOUR RULE HAS ENDED."

Alazaar walks onto the balcony again. His anger grows to new levels as he spots me standing atop a pile of his dead soldiers.

"James. How wrong you are. Today your very life will end," he grumbles to himself. He turns and walks back inside.

The rear gates of the castle opens and Alazaar's army charges through. Sarah's soldier's charge through the front gate. More than four hundred of Alazaar's soldiers against our three hundred plus. Alazaar has the numbers, but not the explosives. Ryan and Captain Krytcher begin throwing balls of rags filled with explosives and rock. They set each on fire as they throw them. The balls contain shards of rock obtained from the creek beds. When they explode, the rocks sear through flesh like arrow heads.

The battle rages: explosions, swords, arrows, shields, men are fighting mortal combat throughout the castle grounds. Ryan and the team rush to the castle underground and set charges where soldiers live and eat. They blow up room after room. Fire breaks out as they fight their way inside the castle proper. Castle rooms can be rebuilt. The objective today is to defeat Alazaar's army. As they make their way, they open the inner doors from inside.

Alexandra is in full battle but sees the inner doors open. She yells, "GEMMA, You're with me."

Gemma slays the soldier in front of her with her sword, her bow and arrows now strapped to her back. She charges forward following Alexander.

I too see the inner doors open, and I want Alazaar. I run fast past soldiers, wielding my sword to their throats as I pass each one.

The three of us fight our way to the throne room. As we pass the ballroom, Gemma spots Morena fleeing. She races after her. Alexandra follows.

"MORENA" shouts Gemma.

Morena stops and turns to face Gemma.

"And so we meet?" laughs Morena. "A slave girl? Oh yes, I've heard all about you. You're the best James could find for a Queen?" she laughs harder.

"Not a slave girl, a humble village girl. We never bothered anyone until you and Alazaar took power. How many people have died because of you?"

"Oh, my dear, the only ones who have died, have been those not strong enough to live. And today you will join their ranks. Such a pity. You would have made a good slave."

Gemma charges for a fight.

Morena exclaims, raising her hand, and speaking she says, "A nal nath rak, doth vie rak nal." The calling of black magic power. With that Gemma is lifted into the air, she flutters as she loses control. With a wave of her arm, Morena sends Gemma flying into the wall, her head hitting the hard stone. She collapses to the floor unconscious.

Morena turns to leave.

"Not so fast you evil witch," exclaims Alexandra. Alexandra stands ready, her sword drawn. Morena again raises her arms. Objects fly toward Alexandra, but she simple knocks them away with her sword. She walks closer and closer to Morena.

Morena calls down more spells and attempts to lift Alexandra as she did Gemma. Alexandra looks at her smugly.

"Your black magic spells have no power over me, witch. Your time of existence has expired." Alexandra thrusts her sword into Morena's abdomen. "Your rule is over."

Morena gasps, "But how? Who are you?"

Blood runs out of Morena's mouth as Alexandra pulls her sword upward, tearing into Morena's heart. Morena expires and collapses to the floor.

Alexandra runs to attend to Gemma. She lifts her in her arms and taps her face, bringing her back to consciousness.

It takes Gemma a moment, but she comes to her senses. She sees Morena's body on the floor. "How?"

She looks at Alexandra.

"James? Where is James?"

James makes his way to the throne room. He fights off several guards and enters. There he eliminates the dignitaries and remaining guards. He stops and turns. Sitting upon the throne is Alazaar.

"Your father taught you well James. A pity he could not join us to watch. Why have you come here James, I have only taken what I deserve. Your father stole my Maria, then he created you with her. Each day I was forced to care for you, knowing your mother was supposed to be with me. I am the one that loved Maria."

"Is that what this is all about? All these years of hatred; I never understood. It's about a romance jealousy from over twenty years ago? My father loved my mother, you never deserved her. You are sick Alazaar."

"Only sick with grief James, for what should have been mine."

"And now I shall have it. I will dispose of your little village girl, and I will hang you in front of everyone."

"I bid you to try Alazaar. You took my mother. You took my father. You took my kingdom. Now, I will take back what is rightfully mine."

I thrust my sword at him and battle ensues. Blades clash as we fight for the right of kingship. Alazaar is strong, but I am fast. We battle for a considerable time. Then in a stroke of luck, I block Alazaar's swing, but he catches me with a blow by his backhand.

The wind is knocked out of me. As Alazaar returns his blade across my abdomen, bloods gushes through my shirt. I fall to the floor.

"It is your time that has ended," he says.

Alazaar comes and sits over top of me.

"You once called me your friend Alazaar."

"You were never my friend James. Only a path to vengeance. I'm not going to hang you; I'm going to kill you right now. And then I'm going to find and kill your pretty little bride."

He raises his sword above my chest.

"NOOOOO!"

Gemma screams from across the room. She races toward Alazaar, drawing and arrow from her quiver. As she runs her rage soars, she snaps the arrow in two, and leaps upon Alazaar's back. In a flash she drives the arrow shaft pieces deep into each side of Alazaar's neck, one piece in each hand. Blood gushes from Alazaar, she grabs his sword and draws it to his neck, and with a quick tug, cuts deep into his throat.

Alazaar collapses.

Gemma pushes his body off of James.

"James, James, talk to me. Don't you die."

She is crying as she pulls me close.

She begins kissing me as I raise my arm and place it around her.

"Gemma," I whisper.

As she feels my arm reach around her and hears my voice she looks at me and lays my head in her lap.

"Hello my love." I caress her check and wipe her tears.

"Oh James, I thought you were gone. I was so scared."

"I'm not leaving you. We have a Kingdom to run - thanks to you. You did it. You killed Alazaar."

She laughs through her tears as happiness slips in hearing my voice again. Gemma sobs as Alexandra walks up behind her. As I hold Gemma in my arm I feel blood running down my side. "Gemma..... bandage," I can barely speak through the pain.

"Oh my goodness," she lifts up and looks at my abdomen. There is a significant slice across my waist. Alexandra grabs the tablecloth and hands it too her. Gemma applies it against my wound. The pain is immense, but her first aid helps stop the bleeding.

A few moments later, Orien, Sarah, and Ryan enter. Alexandra says to Sarah.

"Alazaar is dead. By Gemma's hand."

"So are all his soldiers," exclaims Orien. "The Kingdom is yours again, Your Majesty."

"Gemma and Orien, help me stand. I must go out on the balcony."

"No, James, you need to lay down," says Gemma. "We will get you help."

"No, I need to greet my people. They need to see that I am alive, and that the Kingdom is safe."

They help lift me up, and escort me too the balcony. As we walk out, the crowd cheers at the site of us. I stand staring at the huge crowd of soldiers and towns people, holding on tightly to Gemma and Orien. I look below and see Mark. We wave and smile happily to each other. He salutes me.

Gemma says, "come James, you must lie down."

I nod in agreement, and we make our way to the closest bed. I lay down as Gemma sits beside me.

"It will take a few weeks my love, but you will be fine. Trust me, I know a thing or two about sword wounds to the gut," she says, smiling.

"You saved me." I smile and hold her hand.

"I guess that makes us even then," she replies smiling very happy.

"I love you Gemma."

"I love you too James."

She kisses me passionately.

The End

About the Author: Patrick L. Wimsatt

Patrick is married and has two daughters, two stepdaughters, two stepsons, and a granddaughter. He and his lovely wife reside in Southern Indiana in the United States.

Patrick is a retired United States Air Force Officer achieving the rank of Major, after serving more than 20 years in service to his country. After military service, Patrick returned to college, learning Databases and Software Development, where he continues to work full time in the software industry, supporting the Department of Veteran Affairs for the US Government.

Patrick's first book is/was Gemma. Inspired by several movies starring a popular leading lady, he sat down and wrote Gemma in only six weeks. His love and passion for romance now takes him on a new journey of exciting adventures. One he hopes to continue well into his retirement years.

His most memorable experience during his career was working with a NASA Astronaut and Shuttle Command Pilot who piloted three shuttle missions to space.

www.ingramcontent.com/pod-product-compliance
Lightning Source LLC
Chambersburg PA
CBHW020626110726
47899CB00002B/668